Mrs. Dorri

A Novel.

Volume 3

Mrs. Henry Wayland Chetwynd

Alpha Editions

This edition published in 2023

ISBN : 9789357951333

Design and Setting By
Alpha Editions
www.alphaedis.com
Email - info@alphaedis.com

Contents

CHAPTER I.

Spring struggling through smoke and fog, dingy sparrows playing on the grass, and a careworn face looking upon it all.

The lines left by youth deepen and become more conspicuous in age, and one can generally read the story of the three first decades in the faces of older people. Mrs. Dorriman, suffering in her youth from injustice and a want of affection, bore the marks of both; nothing but her real sweetness of temper had saved her from peevishness, for fretfulness is as much the result of perpetual repression in one feeble by nature, as violence and anger is the outcome of an unchecked temper in youth.

But, as Mrs. Dorriman looked upon the smoky sparrows and the grass showing green under difficulties, she noticed that the birds were contending and not playing, they each wanted a long straw, envied it. Alone they could not lift it, and yet they would not combine their efforts, and after all it had to be left there to the mercy of the wind. Their ineffectual single efforts in so hopeless a cause seemed to the poor little lady typical of humanity, wasting their time struggling for the unattainable, and never seeing how perfectly fruitless are their efforts.

She was roused from this common-place reflection by the entrance of the servant.

Mr. Sandford, better, and busy at his writing-table, had much changed since his last attack. He was rough in manner still, and his speech was imperious because the habit of a lifetime is not easily broken, but in various ways he showed his sister how much he had learned to value her. His own consciousness of not being quite the same—which however he never alluded to openly—the various disappointments he met with in business, the failure of some of his most cherished plans—everything combined to make him cling to his sister as the one object in his life who was always the same, and who never disappointed him.

Though between them lay a secret so important to him, that he perpetually strove to forget it, yet seeing her there by him made him often momentarily forget that anything uncomfortable lay between them.

On her side, his harshness in old days, and the various events of her life in which he had played a part, had been first resolutely pushed away from her and latterly forgotten. Indeed the only feeling she had now was in connection with her husband and that perpetual bewilderment as to its being Christian or right to shrink back from the everlasting companionship which every book she read dwelt upon as offering her the deepest consolation. She had grown fond of her brother, he appreciated her household virtues, and a woman forgives much when she meets with appreciation in what she takes pride in. She had watched the sparrows, and with a quick self-reproach at her own idleness she turned to the door and saw that a telegram was in the servant's hand. One telegram! There were two!

Anxious not to excite Mr. Sandford, she tore one open. It was from Mr. Macfarlane.

"Disastrous fire here and great loss—your papers all safe."

The poor little woman, so suddenly reminded of what she had almost forgotten, felt as though some explosive substance had been thrown at her. In her bewilderment she stretched out the telegram to her brother, forgetting, at the moment, everything except the impulse of having his sympathy, then with a quick flash of remembrance she said, "I did not mean to show it," and held out her hand for it.

Too late! Mr. Sandford had read it, and now with angry and indignant eyes was watching her face.

"What papers are those referred to?" he asked in a harsh voice.

"Papers belonging to my husband—to me. I had forgotten them."

"What are they about?" His voice was harsh and reminded her painfully of old days; something, too, of the fear that held her in such a grasp then came to her now.

"I have not read them."

His brow cleared a little, but he was amazed to find that after all she had not forgotten. They had been so much more to each other lately, so he had thought, and all the time she had held this weapon in reserve to strike him with.

There was so much treachery in this that he was thunderstruck. How little he had sounded the depths of her character, if she was capable of this.

"Brother," she said, "you can tell me what I have never had the courage to find out for myself. Will anything in those papers raise my husband in my estimation, or will they lower him in my eyes?"

"How can I tell what your estimation of your husband is?" he asked, roughly; "he was a kind good-hearted fellow, not a man of business, but thoughtful and good about *you*. You have nothing to complain of."

Nothing to complain of! thoughtful about her! Poor Mrs. Dorriman thought she could not have heard aright. "He left me dependent," she said, with a sob in her voice.

Mr. Sandford shrank, then he said, quickly,

"What have you wanted that you have not had from me?"

"Ah, brother! it is not the same; you do not know how bitter it is to owe everything, to be under an obligation, when it ought not to have been necessary. I should have had my own."

This cry, the outcome of months, and even years, of a perpetual grief to Mrs. Dorriman, was an entirely new light to her brother, whose coarser view of life was that so long as money, food, and clothes were forthcoming it did not matter from whom they came. He was also one of the men who imagine that a woman has no business with money; who conceive that they are not fitted by nature for disposing of any investment or even controlling their income beyond that portion of it allotted to them for the payment of a butcher's bill, or the purchase of some more or less frivolous article of wearing apparel.

He stared at her in silence, conscious that this new phase of her character must be thought over when she was not there. Then he said:

"Write for those papers; there is nothing in them to injure your husband in your eyes. He did think about you."

"Then why did Inchbrae not belong to me? When he told me—at least I *think* he told me—it was mine, and you sold it, how could he think of me and not leave me independent? If Inchbrae was mine how could you sell it and me never consenting?"

"Anne," said Mr. Sandford, "till the papers come we will drop the subject—when they come you will understand. Read the other telegram." He spoke with difficulty, and Mrs. Dorriman in haste opened the yellow missive on her lap, conscious of neglect in another direction. It was from Grace.

"All sorts of complications here—can you not come or send some one who can help Margaret? Her husband ill."

Then all was forgotten but this new anxiety. Mrs. Dorriman felt as though life just now was a great deal too much for her. Her own affairs were of great interest to her—then the papers, her brother, and now Margaret.

"She does not say what sort of help is wanted, and why did Margaret not telegraph herself?"

This was Mr. Sandford; his sister sat thinking and thinking, not coming any nearer a solution, looking helplessly straight before her.

"She has Jean," she said at length.

Mr. Sandford made no answer. He leaned back in his chair thinking, and it was evident from the expression of his face that his thoughts were very painful to him; then he said, slowly:

"There is a man I dislike, and, for the matter of that, he dislikes me, but he is the only person I can think of who can help Margaret just now. His name is Stevens. He was Drayton's manager, and left him because Drayton would not take his advice about an investment I recommended."

"That does not say much for his wisdom," said Mrs. Dorriman, who had a blind belief as regarded her brother's financial capabilities.

"It showed his wisdom," said Mr. Sandford, shortly.

"The investment was a risky one, if not a bad one."

Mrs. Dorriman looked at her brother with wide-open eyes of astonishment.

Mr. Sandford gave a short laugh, in which there was not any mirth. After a moment or two he said,

"Telegraph to this man and ask him to go to Wandsworth at once."

"In your name or mine?" asked Mrs. Dorriman, as she drew a telegraph-form towards her.

"In Margaret's name. Say, 'Mrs. Drayton implores Mr. Stevens to come to her at once. Her husband is very ill.' Put, 'The Limes, Wandsworth.' I think he will act on that," said Mr. Sandford, as he rang the bell and sent the telegram off.

Mrs. Dorriman wrote to Mr. Macfarlane, going out of the room to do so. Her brother's words about her husband were full of mystery to her, but she clung to his saying that her husband had thought of her, and tried not to think of it at all. Soon now she would be made to understand, and, if understanding it all would make her happier, she longed, all the more, for the explanations to be over.

She finished her letter, wondering whether she had said enough and not too much, and sat with the folded and sealed letter between her hands with something of her usual hesitation when she had taken any step of importance. Then she rose quickly and sent it away. She felt she must go into her brother's presence, having fulfilled his wishes. She had not a moment for reflection then, for the front doorbell, usually so silent, rang loudly, and in a moment a tall, broad-shouldered, middle-aged man came into the room and went straight up to her.

"Mrs. Dorriman, I believe? I am told Mr. Sandford is ill, so I asked for you. My name is Stevens," and he shook hands with her and sat down as though sure of his welcome.

"I—we have just telegraphed to you, Mr. Stevens."

"Hah! What about?"

"Mr. Drayton is very ill, and Margaret—we wanted you to go to her."

"Just what I feared," he said; "I had a letter from Sir Albert Gerald, who has been corresponding with me about some Welsh property, some mines, &c.; he said he felt sure Mr. Drayton was too ill to be looked after only by his wife; that he was convinced, from the way he was behaving, that his mind was affected. I came here because I thought I should get full particulars. I am ready to go at once and see if I can be of use."

"Thank you," said Mrs. Dorriman, warmly; "shall I show you the telegram, and would you like to see my brother?"

"I need not disturb your brother. Yes, show me the telegram."

Mrs. Dorriman left the room, leaving Mr. Stevens pacing up and down the room.

"What a horrible shame it was letting any young girl marry him!" he muttered; "and Sandford knew it, for I myself told him."

He took the telegram from Mrs. Dorriman's hand as she entered, and, crumpling it up, he said, "Good-bye," and, before Mrs. Dorriman had fairly realised he was there, he had gone.

She sat down for a moment or two to recover herself, conscious that a powerful help had suddenly been given her in Mr. Stevens.

There was a quickness and decision in his manner which was inexpressibly comforting to her. Knowing very little about him, there was still a mixture of kindness and shrewdness in his face, and a straightforward honesty that impressed her.

She rose to join her brother with half her trouble gone.

"Who has been here?" he asked, as she entered the room.

"Oh, brother, such a wonderful thing! No sooner had my telegram to Mr. Stevens gone than he himself appeared. He had heard something and came to find out what we knew."

Mrs. Dorriman gave a sigh of relief as she sat down.

"Who wrote to him?" asked Mr. Sandford; "does Grace know him?"

"I do not think so; but Sir Albert Gerald wrote. He was corresponding with him on business."

"Sir Albert Gerald?" exclaimed Mr. Sandford; "isn't he the man who was nearly killed at Lornbay?"

"And that Margaret found? Yes," said Mrs. Dorriman.

"What in the world can he be doing there?" said Mr. Sandford; "he had better have kept away."

"But if he helps Margaret?" said Mrs. Dorriman; "it is a great thing for her to have a friend near her."

"That may or may not be," said Mr. Sandford, gloomily; and then, fixing his eyes on his sister, he said, "You are very innocent, Anne, but do you think a young fellow like Sir Albert Gerald a safe friend for a beautiful young girl like Margaret, who is unhappily married?"

"But her marriage was not your doing, you tried to persuade her against it. I said all I could, she has only herself to blame," said Mrs. Dorriman, severely.

"Do not make me more ashamed of myself than I am already," he said, bitterly. "I liked Margaret, and wished to keep her with me. She is like ... but Grace. I did originally persuade him to come here, I did not care about *her*; and I should not have minded her unhappiness. Then I was so angry that I made life unbearable for her; and if evil comes of this can I hold myself blameless?"

He spoke with great agitation, and Mrs. Dorriman felt powerless to say a word to comfort him. She knew that there was truth in his way of putting it, and that in this way he was to blame.

"One thing more," he said, turning suddenly towards her, "and there is no reason now why you should not know it. When I asked Drayton here I did not know what I learnt afterwards from Stevens, and when he told me it was too late; I did not know that his mother died insane, and that he himself had been under restraint. I only knew this after that poor child's marriage, and what could I do?"

A cry of horror burst from Mrs. Dorriman.

"Ah, Anne! You may well be horrified, but can you not see that all this makes me absolutely hate myself? I assure you when I lie down at night, and when I unclose my eyes in the morning, this is the first miserable thought that haunts me, and will haunt me to my dying day."

"Can we do nothing?" she sobbed; "it is so dreadful to think of her so far from us and so helpless."

"If I went there, he would probably be worse, and I confess that his virulent hatred of me is the one fact that reconciles me to being unable to go. Now this man Stevens has gone, he will do more than any one, he has very great influence. I have not the health nor the strength," and, as he sank breathless into a chair, Mrs. Dorriman recognised that this was indeed only too true, and that her place was by his side.

For this agitation brought on one of his worst attacks, and when he was again easier he was as usual feeble and completely prostrated; and sitting beside him, once again as often before, the poor little woman had to bear anxiety patiently, and to fold her hands while all her fears and terrors for Margaret urged her to rush to the scene of action.

Grace neither wrote nor telegraphed, and altogether, perhaps, Mrs. Dorriman had never gone through such a time of trial before.

It seemed to her that her duty lay in two opposite directions, or was it that she could not see quite clearly which was her chief duty?

Things were not much mended by a letter from Jean, who had great pride in her powers of language, and who had the habit of wrapping her meaning in many involved sentences.

"My dear and honoured lady," she wrote, "I am in great distress and anxiety, and Miss Grace is much better and well to do with, and we agree wonderful; and the landlady she is not to be mentioned for meanness and using the oil we pay for, and cooks too bad for any lady to eat, much less a young lady with a high stomach and not strong like Miss Grace, but I don't mind, and I just do things myself and she is well content poor thing, but Miss Margaret's husband has taken a bad turn, and mischief will come and is sure to come if the police will not interfere, and they say they will not because of a law no one understands, and as I have explained this to you, my dear lady, I hope you will forgive me, but I wish you were here, or even Mr. Sandford, as he might show some temper and make them do their duty. I hope Mr. Sandford is well and not very troublesome to do with, though well I know that illness makes everyone a trouble. Look at myself, and a man's worse, so no more from your humble servant, JEAN."

"We hear this bad news from every side," said Mrs. Dorriman, "and I am very anxious, brother."

"There is cause for anxiety, but now Stevens has gone we need not be afraid."

"If he only manages to get in."

"Trust him; besides, you must remember that after all it is only Grace who has been refused admittance."

"That is all we *know* of, but how I wish, how I wish, Margaret was safe here with us!"

"There is no use wishing anything," he said, impatiently. Mrs. Dorriman sighed.

"Is it not true that no good comes of doing anything wrong from however good a motive?"

"What *do* you mean," he said, angrily.

"I mean," she said, hopelessly, "that if Margaret had not wanted to give Grace a home she would not have married Mr. Drayton."

"Do you suppose I do not know that?" he said. "Can you not see that the horror of it all is almost overwhelming me? I have already told you this myself!"

"Oh, brother," said Mrs. Dorriman, remorsefully, "I did not mean ..." Mrs. Dorriman looked ready to cry.

"It is because you do not mean it that it makes it worse. Anne," he said, suddenly raising himself and looking at her, "if any one knew what the word remorse meant, I think there would be less wrong-doing in the world. *It* is the worm that never dies, and the fire that never is quenched." He spoke in a tone of despair and despondency, and Mrs. Dorriman endeavoured to console him.

"You know nothing of this, brother," she said, "you should not speak so. You never did any grievous wrong." She stopped short as a cruel pang of recollection came to her, the haunting fear that once had possessed her. Her face flushed and she trembled visibly.

He looked at her in silence, unable to reconcile to himself the words she spoke, implying trust in him and the doubt expressed in her face. At length he said in a feeble tone, which betrayed the great prostration he was suffering from—

"We will talk another day, Anne. Perhaps when we do have that conversation then you will feel you are free to leave me, to go to Margaret, or any one else."

"Brother," said Mrs. Dorriman, rising and standing beside him with her hands clasped, "I have learned to care for you now—and if in the past anything exists that may part us—let it alone—unless," she added, hastily, "it may be doing my husband's memory a wrong."

She spoke solemnly, and he gazed at her, earnestly.

"I believe you are a good woman, Anne, but you cannot right the one without——"

He waved her away from him, and she, disturbed and agitated, fearing and hoping at one and the same moment, stooped suddenly and kissed him, an unwonted demonstration on her side, but meant as a seal to the promise she had intended to make, and so he understood it.

Mrs. Dorriman, reserved and reticent, had one great hope in all this. She trusted that the story which was so painful in every detail was not known to outsiders. Nothing would seem so painful to her if only they could keep it to themselves. She was one of those people who like to draw her mantle round her and not show her wounds. It is the misfortune of characters like hers that no event ever happens in connection with their home history of an unhappy nature that they do not begin to reproach themselves either for doing or not doing things, or for saying or not saying something in connection with it. A want of self-confidence often leads to a good deal of self-torment, and when she had left her brother's room she was very unhappy, clinging to this one belief of privacy as the one bright spot.

No one need know, and she said these words to herself, and found that they gave her comfort. How long she had sat thinking she did not know, but the twilight was coming on when the servant came to her and asked her if she would receive Mrs. Wymans.

"I am not out, of course, if any one calls; you can show them in," she said, surprised by his tone.

Mrs. Wymans came in with that prepared expression of sympathy that some people feel right to show on all occasions when sorrow may properly be supposed to be in question.

"This is indeed kind," she said, nestling up to Mrs. Dorriman. "I call it real friendship to allow me to see you at such a moment."

"My brother is so much better," said Mrs. Dorriman, with her little air of gentle dignity, "that there is no reason why I should deny myself to any one."

"Ah, so good of you; but then, dear Mrs. Dorriman, I am so deeply interested in you ever since that day we met in the railway-carriage. I have felt so much sympathy and real interest."

"You are very good."

"Oh no! I am not good at all. But your brother, how does he bear it?"

"He is better and in fair enough spirits, considering all things."

"Ah!" and Mrs. Wymans heaved a sigh that might have almost sent a ship across the sea.

The scene was curious—the one woman burning with curiosity and an intense anxiety to know what would put her in the position (in the society of Renton) of being really intimate with Mrs. Dorriman; and the other alarmed, anxious, yet standing bravely up and concealing by a wonderful exertion that she was at all nervous about anything.

"Will he be tried? Of course he will," and Mrs. Wymans heaved another sigh, which was cut short in the middle by want of breath.

Poor Mrs. Dorriman's heart seemed to stand still. Who was meant? Her brother? Still she showed a composed front to Mrs. Wymans, who was perplexed, annoyed, and began to be half afraid her information might not have been correct in every particular.

"You are talking riddles, Mrs. Wymans," and Mrs. Dorriman was unmistakeably annoyed.

"Such strange, such very strange stories spread, one never knows what to believe," Mrs. Wymans answered, "but I heard it on what seemed to be very good authority."

"Would you be so kind as to tell me what you have heard, and in what way it refers to me?" and Mrs. Dorriman felt the suspense was very terrible to her.

"Be prepared, for you evidently have heard nothing," and Mrs. Wymans felt to the full the importance of being the first to tell important news; "Mrs. Drayton's baby is dead, and, Mrs. Dorriman, *the child did not die a natural death*!"

Mrs. Dorriman started—for a moment she lost her self-control.

"Take care, Mrs. Wymans! Oh, do you know what you are saying!"

"You know nothing?"

"I know nothing about the child, and," taking sudden courage at the thought, "Jean, my old servant, wrote to me, and Grace—Miss Rivers—telegraphed, 'Mr. Drayton is ill,' that is all. There is nothing more."

"There is a great deal more. But, my dear Mrs. Dorriman, pray compose yourself; pray do not excite yourself. Mr. Drayton is ill, that is true, but has no one told you anything else?"

"What more can any one have to say?" Mrs. Dorriman asked, struggling for self-command, and feeling as though it was beyond her.

Mrs. Wymans paused; she had believed her authority to be good, and she had so completely credited every word she heard—we are all of us so apt to believe the very worst part of a friend's misfortune—that now, finding that Mrs. Dorriman knew nothing, she began to ask herself, when it was too late, if the story could be altogether true; perhaps it had been exaggerated.

"Perhaps," she said slowly, "as you have heard nothing——"

Mrs. Dorriman turned upon her with a fire and vivacity that fairly astonished her.

"Mrs. Wymans, you have said enough to fill me with apprehension; you say the child is dead. It is strange we do not know this, my brother and I; and you add, in a tone of great meaning, it did not die a natural death. What do you mean?"

Thus brought to bay, Mrs. Wymans blurted out suddenly what she had heard.

"It is said Mr. Drayton is mad, and that he killed the child. For goodness sake, Mrs. Dorriman, do not faint!" she exclaimed, noticing the deadly pallor of the poor little woman before her.

"I——am not going to faint," said poor Mrs. Dorriman, in that far-away voice that speaks of the cruellest mental agitation; "but you have told me a horrible story. I do not believe it!" she continued, with a sob; "but it is horrible, and I must go—I must telegraph at once."

"Yes, do telegraph," said Mrs. Wymans, eagerly; "can I not take the telegram with me? It will hardly be a moment out of my way."

"Thank you, no," said Mrs. Dorriman, coldly.

How little we love the bearer of bad tidings!

"What will you do about Mr. Sandford?" continued the obtuse woman, anxious to be in the way of whatever there was, and not seeing that Mrs. Dorriman was dying to get rid of her; "do make me of use. Shall I go to him? A stranger sometimes breaks bad news better than a very near relation."

Mrs. Dorriman's patience was at an end.

"You must prove that your news is true," she said, "before venturing to condole with my brother or with me; and Mrs. Wymans—we know each other very slightly, and I must ask you to be so very kind as to leave me."

Mrs. Wymans, a woman upon whom it was very difficult indeed to make any impression, was, for once in her life, completely taken aback by the sudden assertion of herself in a woman she had looked upon as an amiable fool. Her farewells were uttered with rapidity, and she left the room and the house quite unable to comprehend how her visit had failed, or why it was she was made to feel that her intrusion was an impertinence. Mrs. Dorriman, left alone, tried to collect her thoughts and not to take this story for granted. If it was true, even that the child was dead, why did not Grace or Jean or some one telegraph?

All at once what she had dreaded and expected came to her—once again a telegram was brought to her.

"Poor Margaret in frightful distress—her child is dead—scarlet fever."

The relief of this last information, after all she had dreaded, broke her down. She sobbed for some moments very piteously.

Then she went to Mr. Sandford and astonished him by the way she put the matter before him.

"It is such a relief!" she began, incoherently, and not telling him what the relief was: then she added, the tears rolling over her face, "Poor Margaret's child is dead!"

Mr. Sandford was shocked, but failed to understand why this news, which affected him so slightly, was a relief.

"Was anything wrong about the child?" he asked.

"Wrong with it?"

"Yes; why is its death a relief to you?"

"Oh, brother!" she answered, hysterically, "Not its death—but the way it died."

He understood that some worse fate had been suggested to her, and he tried to console her—

"I have seen copies of all the correspondence that took place when Drayton was under restraint before," he said, "and it distinctly says that he was obstinate and very troublesome, but never violent."

Mrs. Dorriman tried hard to think this was consoling but failed to do so.

The horror of it was almost unbearable, and she left the room unable to face any discussion about it, even with her brother; utterly and entirely wretched, and longing to be able to see any one element of consolation in the position, for Margaret's sake.

CHAPTER II.

At the Limes the position of affairs became more terrible every day for Margaret. Mr. Drayton was always sullen, silent, and watchful, and the incessant watchfulness broke down her nerves. She had long fits of crying, without herself being aware of it. The women-servants had left, and she could not replace them; the one woman who came by day to clean and cook (and could do neither) was the only one besides her nurse, and Margaret lived in dread of her leaving her.

There came a day when Mr. Drayton had a very terrible outbreak with the man, who up till now had got on with him. And the scene ended in his also going—telling Mrs. Drayton that he had been engaged to look after an inebriate, and not a madman.

"You think him mad?" faltered Margaret, looking anxiously at him, a ray of hope coming to her. If this man who had experience thought so, might he not convince the doctors?

"I think so; at least I know he is mad at times. No man in his senses would go on as he has done," and the man smoothed out his collar regardless of Mrs. Drayton's presence. "You see he is very dangerous and very cunning, and that's where it is. You might have any number of doctors to see him, and before them he controls himself so that no one would believe him to be what he is. I never was treated so before," and he smoothed his hair and prepared to leave her.

"Can you not stop?" whispered Margaret, in greater agitation; "I—I am frightened."

"I cannot stop because now he's took against me," he answered, "and he shouts the moment he sees me. I've lost all control of him, and my staying would do no good to you or to no one else."

Poor Margaret looked despairingly at him, and, a little moved by her expression, he said briskly—

"Don't you be afraid, ma'am. I'll go straight to the doctor; he sent me here, and he knows me, and I'll tell him exactly what it is, and he'll come first thing and see him."

Margaret saw him go, with absolute despair. She had suffered very much lately; her baby who slept with her had been so fretful and so very sleepless.

The poor child herself had no experience, and the nurse she had was a young woman who was good-tempered and kind, but not skilful. For several nights the child had never slept except in Margaret's weary arms, as she walked up and down, and up and down with it. Each time she tried to lay it down it woke and cried, and, like all children accustomed to being much fondled and carried about by its mother, it disliked being handed over to the nurse when it was ill.

The want of sleep, the incessant terror she was in, all she went through with those terrible tireless eyes always upon her, everything combined to make her really ill.

The strain became intolerable, and Margaret recognised that something must be done—some one must interfere in her behalf and take her and her child away.

Only through her nurse could she hear of Grace. Jean went repeatedly to the house, and never succeeded in baffling Mr. Drayton's watchfulness. Now the man-servant had gone he never opened the door, and the bells might ring all day long, he took no notice. More than once Margaret glided to the door trusting to give a message, to hear a voice she knew, only to feel a hard grip upon her shoulder, and to be thrust back.

The stone passage between the gate and the house was too long for her to make herself heard. She could not understand why Grace sent no message and why no letters reached her—and only found out long afterwards that her cook, who not unnaturally found the place anything but what she liked, spent her time in going to London and looking for another situation, and never went near Grace at all.

It was as well that the poor thing did not know then what a broken reed she was trusting to.

She hoped much from the man's statement to the doctor, and as she walked up and down, and up and down through the long and weary night, she tried to think that soon this terrible state of matters would end for her and for her child.

From the nursery window she could look over the trees and shrubs, and over the high wall into the distance, and she envied the people going to and fro. She had committed no crime, and yet she was, to all intents and purposes, a prisoner. She had no society, no friends, no books; and when she made an effort over herself, and met her husband at the ill-served dinner—he never spoke to her; when she encountered him occasionally in the passage—he was equally silent, but the fierce expression of his eyes terrified her, and she avoided those meetings, creeping back sometimes with a fear of him that increased daily.

The warmer weather now kept her almost all day in the garden, where Mr. Drayton never cared to come, and where she felt free.

But each day increased her trouble now about her child. It lay feverish and breathless at times. If she roused it and tried to get it to play with her it cried, and at length even her experienced eyes saw that it was more than a passing indisposition.

Alarmed, she rushed to her husband's sitting-room. He was sitting as usual near the window, and talking, she thought, to some one, but on going up to the window she found he was alone and talking to himself. There was something so terrible to her in the imaginary conversation he was holding, that for one moment she drew back frightened, even more than usual, but her mother's love gave her courage and she went up to him.

"Baby is ill," she said, very earnestly. "Poor baby! I have no experience. Will you let me have the doctor?"

"No," he answered, angrily. "No; it is only a trick, you played me a trick the other day, and I allow no one to come here again. You are my wife and no one shall come to see you."

"It is not to see me," she said, trembling, trying to humour him, "it is baby. Oh! you will let me send for the doctor?"

"No doctor or other man shall come here," he said with fury; "I know you now, you are full of tricks, and if a doctor came you would tell him."

"I would tell him about my baby!" she cried. "Oh, if ever you cared for me, if ever you loved me, you will let me see a doctor for my child!"

He watched her for a moment or two, with half-closed eyes, cunningly, triumphantly, and curiously, and then he pushed her out of the room.

She rushed to the front door and beat helplessly upon it with her hands, and he heard her, and came out and tried to stop her, on her way upstairs.

"If you try and leave the house I will lock you up," he said, maliciously; "and your pretty baby may cry its eyes out, but you shan't see it."

A new terror sent her flying upstairs to its side.

The nurse, frightened and grieved, volunteered to go, whatever happened.

"But he may not let me in when I come back," she added.

To Margaret, watching her child suffer, what did this matter?

"Go!" she exclaimed; "fly, and if you can tell my sister. My God!" she exclaimed, "send some one to help me;" she sank on her knees, her arms still round the child, and the woman vanished.

The moments seemed hours to her, to raise and fan its little face, to try and get it to swallow a few drops to cool its parched mouth, to lull it in her arms and shower kisses on the feet and hands. How long she was with it alone she did not know, but she was startled by the door opening. She had forgotten to lock herself in!

She knew it was her husband! He came and leaned against the wall, looking at her.

"No one can come in," he said. "I am complete master of the situation," and then he gave one of his most terrible laughs.

The baby lying half soothed in a short slumber started violently and convulsions came on. Margaret, driven to frenzy, threw open the window and shrieked till the whole place rang with her despair.

"Help!" she screamed, "for my baby is dying."

Mr. Drayton still stood repeating the same terrible sentence, and then laughing.

Help was hurrying towards her though she did not know it. The little form clasped to her heart became suddenly still, and the wings of angels swept through the room—those angels who come so often as a blessing though they strike terror to our blinded eyes. Suddenly the baby's eyes unclosed—a lovely smile came to the flushed face; stretching out its arms, it said in its childish broken words, "Lovely, mother, lovely!" and then, turning its head aside, went with them.

Four people, appalled by the stillness of the house, made an entrance. Margaret's cries for help had been heard, but those cries had long ceased, the intense quietness and still was not broken even by Mr. Drayton.

Something had subdued him. Even on his diseased brain the influence of that dread presence was felt; he crouched in a corner, and wondered why Margaret was so quiet, and why she did not speak to the child.

They found him so crouched. Jean and Mr. Stevens were first, Jean's warm heart full of deepest compassion; then came the two medical men Mr. Stevens had brought with him, one of whom had had charge of Mr. Drayton in former days.

Margaret was still insensible when she was carried downstairs. Kindly hands tended to her needs, and when she woke from this prolonged unconsciousness it was to lie still and never speak. The shock had been so appalling that it had apparently numbed her senses. She asked no questions and never spoke even of her dead baby.

She took what was offered to her passively, but nothing elicited a change of expression. They took her to cheerful rooms engaged by Mr. Stevens for her and her sister. Grace, whose health seemed so much better now that there was necessity for her exerting herself, was in despair.

"Will she ever recover?" she asked, in anguish, of the kind and clever man who visited her so regularly. "Will my sister ever know me again?"

"I believe she will. It would be a great matter if she could cry—a good hearty cry might do much for her."

"I don't know how to make her," said Grace, in accents of despair.

"But I do, ma'am," said Jean. "I cut the poor bonny boy's hair off, and we had him photographed. I will show her the picture, and then tears will come."

"Give me the hair," said the doctor, hastily, and he took it quickly out of the room with him.

When they next met Grace asked him about it.

"Why did you carry it off, doctor?"

"Because the poor child died of suppressed scarlet fever," he answered, "and I took it to be disinfected."

"That's a new name for an ill deed," said Jean.

"It's quite true—the child's throat showed what it died of," he said.

"It died of neglect," said Jean, obstinately. "How was the poor young thing to know how to deal with it? Fever or no fever, the man's a cruel-hearted man, and shall never come near her again."

"You say a truthful thing in saying that," said the doctor, in a low voice. "Mr. Drayton died this morning."

"No!" exclaimed Grace. "He seemed such a strong man when I last saw him," and she shuddered, for since the days when she had laid ill and had urged Margaret to marry him for her own selfish ends she had never seen him to speak to, excepting once.

Jean was silent. There was a verse in her heart but she would not say it out just then.

"He was a violent man," said the doctor. "It is quite dreadful to think of that poor child in such a man's power. He had a terrible attack of passion in the asylum—a blood-vessel in the brain gave way, and all was over in a few minutes."

"There are so many things I cannot understand," said Grace, who felt those last days too much to speak about them. "Surely Margaret must have consulted a doctor. Why did he not interfere? He must have seen that that wretched man was insane."

"Ah," said the doctor, rising, and not choosing to say to her what he had said to Doctor Jones, "medical men are not always infallible."

"They are human creatures," said Jean—"poor erring mortals."

To Doctor Jones—the great man from London spoke plainly, albeit with a politeness which was very chilling.

"We cannot understand, sir, your not having recognised the man as a dangerous lunatic, but probably you have not had much experience of this kind."

"I was beginning to be uneasy," stammered Doctor Jones, who had appeared on the scene because the man he had sent there had warned him that there would probably be murder, and that he would get into a scrape if he did not interfere in some way.

"Were you?" said Doctor Plunkett, an Irishman, with all the sense of fun of a typical Irishman of the best class; "were you really? You had begun to think you had made a mistake." Then he added, in a more serious tone, "Doctor Jones, it is a very serious matter."

"I think it is very serious."

"What made you so *determined* not to see that the unfortunate man was out of his mind?"

"How do you know I was determined, sir?" said Doctor Jones, anxiously.

"Because Miss Rivers, in stating the case, told me you had made up your mind beforehand!"

"I—I thought that Mrs. Drayton was——well, not quite straightforward."

"That has nothing whatever to do with it. If we medical men are to judge of a patient's condition because we like or dislike their relations there is an end of everything," Doctor Plunkett said severely; "surely a case must be judged on its own merits?"

"Of course, sir, of course. My wife, sir——"

Doctor Plunkett looked at him in amazement.

"You do not mean to say, sir," he said, in a tone of cutting contempt, "that you allow your *wife* to dictate to you upon a subject she can know nothing about?"

Doctor Jones felt utterly crushed.

When Doctor Plunkett was leaving the room the unhappy little man got near him and said, in a tone of abject entreaty,

"I do trust, sir, that, if you have conceived an unfavourable opinion of me in this matter, you—will—perhaps, sir, you will not speak of it anywhere. It would ruin me, sir, in the eyes of my wife."

"Sir," said Mr. Plunkett, "we medical men are supposed to stand by each other, but a man who is in subjection to his wife has no business to be a doctor, in my opinion." He added, "I think a henpecked man is an error in existence. I do not think he has any right to exist at all," and he left Dr. Jones to digest this speech as best he could.

It was getting much warmer, though the spring was not yet far on: That wonderful promise of a coming fulness, which is one of the great charms of spring, made itself felt, but as yet the days were not long, and Grace, impatient and restless, wanted Margaret to know what had passed; she wished her to know she was free.

Now that Mr. Drayton was dead, the sister who had been, for a time, bowed with remorse, tried to shake it off. It had been terrible, and the death of the little one, that perhaps might have been saved, was too sad.

But now it was all over why should not Margaret revive? why could she not speak and break a silence that was becoming so very terrible?

Grace had not much more comprehension now than she had had in old days of the depths of her sister's nature; and she did not know in its entirety what Margaret had suffered in those months of anguish and seclusion.

Perhaps the person who best understood her was Jean, whose own deep warm feelings taught her sympathy.

And Jean in those days was invaluable. She shielded Margaret from every intrusion, she cared for her, tended her, and prayed for her; and she sometimes thought as she stood beside her in the stillness of the night—when with her head bowed and her hands clasped she prayed in the old Bible words so familiar to her, and so strange to the poor prostrate girl—that there was a look of tears in the dim, half-closed eyes, and she had hope.

It was a quiet place where they were, and Margaret's room looked out upon a wide flower-garden. As the trees began to show green, none of the surrounding houses could be seen, and Grace used to bring in every favourite flower she knew her sister had in old days loved.

The window was open, and as Jean sat near it, busy with her knitting, a few birds, accustomed to be fed, came to the window-sill and pecked cheerfully, if a little disdainfully, at food they no longer required.

A slight movement from the bed made her turn quickly, and she saw that Margaret's eyes were more fully opened than they had yet been, and that she was looking curiously and strangely at her.

Jean, with one of her inward and fervent prayers, went to the bed, and laid within reach and sight of her the golden curls she had treasured for her, and the photograph of the little child—then she turned away.

With the feeblest hand and a faint cry Margaret took these things up and passed them through her fingers in an uncertain hesitating way, then she looked at the picture....

The child lay in that stiller rest as though about to awaken, flowers were around it, and on its face was the smile with which it had left her.

In a moment Jean heard the welcome sound of tears and a sob, and rising quietly she shut the window and left the room, knowing just then solitude was best.

Margaret was saved: day by day she began now to rally, her words were still whispers from the extremity of her weakness, but she began to listen and notice and answered; still, to Grace's impatient eyes, the progress was slow.

They told her of Mr. Drayton's death, but no one could fathom her thoughts about it. Grace worried Jean every hour and every moment of the day. "It seems so hard, Jean, now all is over, why can she not be as she used to be?"

"She never will be that, my bairn," said the old woman, "she will bear a scar all her days in her heart. It will heal, but there will be the mark. A wound like that is not a thing that can be blotted out altogether."

"You know, I never saw the baby," said Grace.

"It is not only the loss of the baby, that's sore, but a sense of having sinned, that's helping to keep her down," said Jean; "she feels that she has done evil that good may come, and we are commanded not to do that. And her nerves are nearly gone. You do not realize, my dear, all that poor thing has suffered. I tremble, myself, when I think of her, month after month, in the power of the poor madman. It's awful, Miss Grace, you must just be patient and pray for her too."

Mrs. Dorriman's letters were now addressed to Margaret, and showed to no one.

But one day she said to Jean, "When the doctor next comes, Jean, we will ask him when I may go to Scotland," and the old woman was delighted, for to her to be so far from Mrs. Dorriman, and not a "kent face" near her, was a trial.

Another subject that amazed Grace a good deal was the apparent desertion of Sir Albert Gerald and Mr. Paul Lyons.

Sir Albert having effected poor Margaret's release was full of remorse because that release had been so late, though he was conscious of not having lost time when he had fully grasped the situation; he still mourned over the death of the poor child, whose life might have been saved under ordinary circumstances. He understood Margaret better than most of those round her, and he knew that if ever, in the future, he hoped to see her, he must keep away now.

Grace was exceedingly amazed when she received a letter from him—from Spain; true he entreated her to write to him, but his having gone so far off was tiresome.

Then Mr. Lyons, he neither came nor wrote, and altogether Grace thought now, as she once had done before, it is always Margaret.

Still there were consolations in her present lot; she appreciated to the full having the command of money, and this was supplied unsparingly by Mrs. Dorriman at her brother's wish.

He was not, in any way, a man who grudged money, and he was one of the men who had a vague idea that most things, even a broken heart, could be mended by a cheque.

He was more relieved by Mr. Drayton's death than any one, and horrified his sister by saying so.

"It is a terrible thing you say, Anne; now I call that humbug; what is the use of pretending to grieve?"

"He might have recovered," she said, gently; "and brother, I do not think it is right to rejoice over any one's death."

"Who says I rejoice?"

"You look as if you did."

"Well, it is a relief; and in this world so seldom the right person seems to die...."

"Oh, hush!" she said, inexpressibly shocked and distressed.

"Anne, I know you try to be honest, but you have a crooked way of looking at things."

"I do not think I have, and," she added, plucking up a little spirit, "you have no right to say so; and the subject is so terribly painful to me, I thought it would be equally painful to you."

"You don't understand the question," he said, with something of his old violence. "I am ready to destroy myself when I think I ever gave that man an opportunity of seeing poor Margaret, and now that he is gone I cannot pretend to regret him. His death has ended a terrible complication."

"I cannot follow your way of thinking," Mrs. Dorriman said, feeling somehow that this did not sound right.

"Well, you had best leave me just now, and when you have quite disentangled your ideas we can renew the subject. I never knew such a brain as yours, it seems to be generally in a hopeless state of muddle about everything." This complimentary speech nearly reduced her to tears, and she hurried from the room only to be immediately called back.

"I am a brute and you must forgive me, Anne," he said; "and there is another thing I want to speak to you about."

His voice sounded strange to her, and looking at him she saw that he was agitated.

"Say nothing just now to distress or worry yourself, brother," she said, quickly.

He took no notice of her, he tapped the table before him with a massive paper-cutter, then he said in an odd tone,

"What were you saying to-day about Margaret's coming to Scotland?"

"The doctor wants her to have sea air and Scotch air, she wishes to come."

"Here?"

"No, not here. Somewhere (she does not care where) she has never seen. Some place, with no recollections clinging to it.

"Lornbay?"

"She has been there. No! not Lornbay."

"How would Inchbrae do?" her brother asked as he watched her face closely.

Her colour came and went, then her eyes filled with tears.

"Alas! that is out of the question."

"Is it?" He seemed to speak with a sudden sense of difficulty.

"Anne," he said at length, "have you really never guessed, never thought, that Inchbrae could not be sold? Do you know so little really of any business matters as not to know that without your consent, without many formalities, the place, which is your place, could not be sold?"

"Not sold! and the place is really mine?" said the poor woman, feeling naturally more bewildered than ever.

"Yes, it is yours," he said, trying to cover his sense of shame by speaking carelessly. His feelings towards his sister were so much altered now, that looking back upon the brutality and roughness with which he had moulded her fate gave him a pang he never would have believed in former days. And there was something else, there was a page in his history which often haunted him now. The burden of knowing it even, could not be anything but painful to him, and the pain grew now each day more and more intolerable.

Mrs. Dorriman was essentially a woman who had no self-confidence, she hesitated over even small matters, and was so afraid of presumption and other sins that she said what she felt right at times, impelled by a directness and a sincere love of truth to say it abruptly, and having done this repented her sharpness with undue humility and apologised for being obliged to say what she thought.

But living in the perpetual companionship of a woman who was so utterly unselfish and so unworldly, a woman whose candour and transparency were those of a child, was an experience that told even upon Mr. Sandford's blunt perceptions.

He had learned to value her, and just as he knew that she had become much to him he had to lower himself probably for ever in her eyes.

Mrs. Dorriman was at this moment perturbed, distressed, and excited beyond conception. To have been peremptorily taken from her own home and her people ... to have been deceived! Then swiftly came the remembrance that she had been led to wrong her husband's memory. Thoughts pressed upon her that were nearly intolerable to her, and she left the room, going to her own, where she tried to bring her thoughts into order.

Why had her brother done this? It was not then that he cared for her, for she knew well that in those days (that now seemed so far away) he had cared for her very little.

Poor woman! her new affection for him seemed suddenly swept away since he could carry out so much deception towards her.

It was so cruel to leave her all this while blaming her husband; and till lately, when he had spoken of his having "taken care" of her, she had seen nothing but unkindness in the way she had been left dependent.

Sudden enlightenment came as a flash to her; those papers she had kept were of real consequence, and opened up the history of her brother's past. She had, as we know, more than once thought of this—or rather nearly thought it out, and pushed the feeling back with a kind of terror.

To be certain that she had no weapons to strike him with he had broken up her home—to have her near him and watch her actions.

She rose suddenly from her chair: she felt suffocating with the pressure upon her mind. How could she forgive him? She walked quickly up and down her room, her hands clasped closely; then she said aloud, "My husband, forgive me," and then cried, poor thing, till she exhausted herself.

The twilight came on; the factories, so grim by day, blazed out with their myriad lights.

Mrs. Dorriman could not go down; she could not yet forgive. She had some food sent to her, and then prepared to go to bed.

Taking up her Bible mechanically she read and took in nothing she saw; she shut it again and tried to say her prayers. Was there not something about forgiving trespasses that she said twice every day?

There was a severe mental struggle, and it was dark when it was over. She went slowly to her brother's room. He was awake.

"Brother," she said, going up to him and laying her hand upon his, "I have come to say that I forgive!"

CHAPTER III.

Nothing could exceed Grace's disappointment when she found that, though Margaret rallied, got up, moved about, went out, and in all ways seemed to be her old self as far as bodily health went, she remained grave, quiet, and apparently indifferent to the various plans and arrangements proposed by her sister.

Grace began to know what we most of us live to find out, that something we have longed for—perhaps unduly—is given to us in a manner that makes us often regret the time and thoughts we have wasted upon it.

From the time she had been old enough to wish for anything, she had wished to be in or near London to see and be seen. First, she had been very ill herself, and now, here was Margaret, a widow and childless, and her dreams must equally vanish. At the beginning she had been filled with remorse, then she got a little weary of trying to sympathise, knowing that it was only trying, now she got very impatient.

Margaret had heaps of money, why could she not drive a little, or do something more than pace that tiresome little garden, read dull books, and go to a little grave?

Her joy may be conceived when one day Margaret was asked if she would see Lady Lyons. It was, at all events, some one who was neither a doctor or a nurse.

Lady Lyons, unaccustomed to more than a general friendliness on the part of her friends, from being a little deaf and not a little tiresome, was immensely flattered by the excuses Grace made for Margaret, and her evident pleasure at her visit; her one unflattering reflection being that she trusted this open satisfaction had nothing to do with her son and any advances he might have made in this direction.

Margaret had been her desire previously, when her inheritance was only problematical. Imagine what her wishes were now when every one knew that Margaret was a very rich widow.

She endeavoured to meet Grace with a friendliness that committed her to nothing, and her talk was of Margaret, and ever Margaret. Was she getting over the sad, she might say the mysterious, death of the child?

"There was nothing very mysterious about it. It died of suppressed scarlet fever, poor little thing. I never saw it. No, Margaret is not getting over it. She never smiles, and at night she cries often. Lady Lyons, I do wish she would get over it; I do find it so terribly dull."

"I dare say," said Lady Lyons, without any show of sympathy.

"Day after day not a soul, save and except the doctor, and he is always in too great a hurry to be pleasant," and Grace gave a long sigh. "When I heard your name it was such a godsend. Do you know I positively have not spoken to a soul for days and days, except Margaret and that old Scotchwoman, who is stark staring mad on religious subjects."

"But you have the comfort of being with your sister," said Lady Lyons, a little stiffly.

"She does not want me in the very least," said Grace, eagerly, a plan developing itself quite suddenly in her fertile brain; "not in the very least. No, Lady Lyons, what I mean to do is——How long must I wear this?" she said, suddenly touching the crape on her dress.

"Oh, Miss Rivers! You being Scotch makes such a difference; in England mourning is less and less worn as it used to be, and now people take to kilting crape it takes away from the blackness of it somehow. In Scotland you would have to wear it months and months, and as you are Scotch——"

"I am only Scotch on one side of my house," exclaimed Grace, "and I do not intend to shut myself up for months and months. No, Lady Lyons, I have a plan, but I do not see much use in telling it to you, if you think I am going to dress like a mute at a funeral."

"I am sure I do not wish to hear your plan," said Lady Lyons, irritated by Grace's manner and by her words, "I came to call upon your sister; will you be so good as to say that sincere sorrow for *her* made me lay aside my invalid habits and come out."

"Please don't go," said Grace, "and for goodness sake don't talk about being an invalid. I have not a lung left, so they say, or only a little bit of one, and I will not be ill or anything. Now I will tell you what I mean to do. I mean to go to London, and pay a good deal of money to some great lady, and go about with her as soon as I decently can."

"My dear Miss Rivers, no very great lady would care to do this; they want nothing you can give them."

"Well then a smaller one must do," said Grace calmly; "but she must know everybody, heaps of people and all that—she must be in the swim you know."

"But I do not know," said Lady Lyons. "In the swim! What do you mean? I have not the faintest idea."

"Oh, Paul will know."

(It had already come to this: she called him Paul! Lady Lyons was extremely displeased.)

"My son, whom you call 'Paul,'" she said, stiffly, "what can he do? He is but young."

"Oh, he knows the world a little though he is young; of course I call him Paul."

"He does know the world," said the irritated mother, "I hope he knows the world too well to be a victim to any one who is not ... in a position I should like."

"You are quite wrong, dear Lady Lyons; being a man of the world, and knowing the world a little, are two very different things, and no one can call Paul a man, he is so very young; that was what I said to him only the other day. And about a position you would like, you mean your son must marry for money. Now, I have too good an opinion of Paul to believe it—and no one worth his salt will choose only to please his mother."

"I am so unaccustomed to hear such ... unfeminine sentiments," and the irate Lady Lyons rose to go.

"It is very good for every one to hear several sides to any question," said Grace, rising also; "I hope I have not offended you, Lady Lyons; but you know I am one of the people who never can help speaking the truth upon all occasions—more especially when it suits me," she added to herself.

"You have not offended me at all," answered Lady Lyons, very much ruffled; "the opinion of a young lady who does not know the world has not so much weight as you think."

"Now, you want to be disagreeable," said Grace, laughing, "and you need not try. When I was in a scrape at school, which was very seldom, the good people did not know what to do, because scolding I never minded a bit, and hard sayings never hit me, so you see I am a hopeless character—but for Margaret, perhaps, no one would ever speak to me. She is very different."

"Yes, she is very different. I think she must be curiously different. Do you never vex her, Miss Rivers? Have you never wounded her sensibilities?"

The quick colour, even tears, came suddenly into Grace's usually tearless eyes. She tried hard to hide them, but Lady Lyons saw them, and they melted her a little. "Ah!" she said, "Yes. Well, a sincere and warm affection for your sister may bring out your good qualities."

"Thank you," said Grace, demurely, rapidly regaining her usual spirits. And when Lady Lyons went away she carried with her a most confused impression of the girl who had made fun of her at one moment and shown very bad taste in talking about Paul with so much familiarity, and the next betrayed very deep feeling for her sister.

Lady Lyons was one of the many people in the world who forget that, though the influence of civilization has a levelling effect, underneath are many varieties of character, and that the most ordinary is a complex one, not wholly good or wholly bad, but partaking of both.

In a different way there was another person who had at first given fullest sympathy to Margaret's desolation, and yet who also now felt that she was becoming morbid in her grief, and who wished to see her rousing herself from it.

This was Jean.

With all the depth of a nature both intense and passionate she had felt the death of the little child for her, as she had felt all the horrors she had gone through.

But now she saw that Margaret was nursing and indulging her sorrow, and she was anxious to wean her from its perpetual contemplation, conscious, through the fine natural instinct that belonged to her, that if the habit of solitude, of mourning, and of shrinking from all companionship, was once formed, it would be far more difficult to break through it afterwards.

The visits to the little grave, where each flower was laid and watered with tears, must be used to turn her thoughts to living children in great need of a share of her sympathy and of her help.

With her Bible in her hand, and a hearty prayer in her heart, the faithful old woman accompanied Margaret, as she had often done before, to the little corner, where the poor young mother wept and meditated, recalling every broken lisping word, so dear to her, and losing herself in fond remembrance of her lost darling.

"My bairn," said Jean, when the fresh flowers had been laid down, and Margaret stood like a frail shadow in her long black robes, "have you ever thought how much money you have now in your hands to spend?"

"Oh! do not speak of it here," said Margaret, shocked and distressed.

"Why should I not speak of it here?" said Jean, stoutly; "it is here that I want to show you that you should do something with it."

"I shall never claim it, never spend it!" exclaimed Margaret, twining her thin white fingers round the little marble cross close to her.

"But you must do both," said Jean, emphatically. "You must claim the money, and spend the money. You must spend it, my dear, for the glory of God, and to give help."

"How? Tell me how can I?"

"You never can, if you do not look further than to a few feet of green turf, and allow nothing else to fill your mind. Look round you, my bairn; see where others suffer. You mourn most because you think that if help had come your child might have lived."

"It might," murmured Margaret, in a suffocated voice.

"And, if you think that, there are hundreds and thousands of children who die because they cannot get the help you might give them, having the means."

"What do you mean, Jean?" and Margaret was startled into momentary forgetfulness.

"Oh, my bairn! you have but to walk in the streets of the Great Babylon and see the poor little things; but go out of the streets; go into the byways; leave the highways alone and see for yourself. When I lost my way the day I took a letter from you to the bank I saw a sight that set my heart aching; and, as I saw all the filth and misery, I took comfort to myself, and said, 'My young lady is rich, and she will do something for these little ones.'"

"But anything I could do would be such a drop in the ocean."

"And is the ocean not made up of drops? We can all do but little—but must we not see we do that little?"

"How can I begin?"

"I am a poor ignorant body, but I would go to some doctor and say—'I do not want this money, but I want to help children, for the sake of a little child I loved and lost myself."

Margaret's tears were falling, but they were not tears of bitterness. Jean had touched a right chord. With the possibility of doing something, an incentive for action given, came a glow of warmer feeling for humanity. The selfishness of her sorrow grew less, and, as she once again knelt in prayer beside the flower-covered grave, she did not pray for herself only, for that meeting she longed for, but she prayed also for others, and rose up filled with a sincere hope that she might be a comfort and help to them in the future.

She walked quietly and silently by Jean's side. No more passed between them; but when they reached home she stopped in the hall, and, putting her arms round Jean's ample shoulders, she kissed her heartily.

Full of her new resolve, Grace's mood jarred not a little upon Margaret; but she meant honestly to try for less selfishness. She had owned to herself she was selfish, and she bravely tried to turn her whole attention to her sister's enthusiastic account of no less an important matter than a brown velvet dress, which had completely taken possession of her imagination.

"How long do you want me to wear this, darling?" she asked, with an air as though, however repugnant to her own feelings, she was prepared to make a sacrifice on her sister's account.

A little while ago, only a few hours ago, how poor Margaret would have shrunk from such a question? Now it was with a fond touch on Grace's shoulder that she said, softly,

"I have been selfish, dear. I have expected you to mourn with me; you have no memory of my child. No, do not wear the semblance of a sorrow you cannot feel."

"You are a darling, Margaret. Then I may have the velvet?"

"Is it very costly?" asked Margaret, trying hard to enter entirely into the interests of the moment with Grace.

"Not for *you* to give me," said Grace, as she twirled round the room, enchanted at this first grand success of her newly-formed resolution.

Margaret looked at her in surprise.

"You talk as though you expected me to use ... his money for you and for myself."

"Good gracious, Margaret, you are surely not going to be ridiculous about it! And I wanted you to do so many things for me. I had set my heart upon going to London and upon having nice things; you are too bad!" and Grace, whose hopes were so suddenly dashed to the ground, burst out crying.

Margaret was infinitely pained. Apart as she was in feeling from Grace, she yet was conscious of a perpetual disappointment in connection with her character that seemed to chill her. And it was very wonderful, she thought, because Grace had been very ill and near the gates of the eternal life, and such an illness must be, in some ways, like a great sorrow, and must surely have made the trivial vanities of life seem trivial indeed. But, as she spoke of wealth, she must make her understand that she could not use any of *his* money, except in some way to help others in need of help.

"Grace," she said, sitting down and drawing her sister towards her, "I want you to listen to me, and I wish you to understand."

"I will not listen," answered Grace, still sobbing violently, "if you are going to be horrid. You cannot imagine my disappointment! I thought, once you got better and ... forgot, that it would be all right again, and that I should do what I like and go where I liked, and all that, and how can I if you will not give me any money?"

"Nothing will induce me to spend any of my husband's money on myself or upon you, Grace. You do not know my feeling about it. I sinned in marrying him, and I should perpetuate the sin if I spent his wealth upon me and mine. I cannot go through what I once did, and now that I see everything more clearly I cannot act against my conviction."

"Then what is the use of your having sacrificed yourself?" asked Grace, in a tone in which anger and contempt were mingled; "really, Margaret, you are so high-flown and so ridiculous! Of course, taking it in that way, one would not expect you to do the thing again. I never should dream of asking you, but, having done it, what is the use of undoing all the good of it?"

"The good of it! Oh, Grace, do not speak of it; it cuts me to the heart, dear, that you, my own sister, cannot understand me better, that you cannot see that evil, and not good, came of it!"

"Of course," said Grace drying her eyes, "the poor little child's death is an evil to you, and I assure you whenever I think of it I could cry. Don't think, because I don't want to wear black, that I am not as sorry as I can be: but now that dreadful man is dead why should you not be comfortable again?"

Margaret sprang from her seat and stood opposite her sister; her countenance was lit up with a sort of passionate sorrow and regret.

"Do you not understand something—a little of what I feel? Do you know, Grace, that when that little life was given to me I thought nothing signified. I neglected that poor, unhappy man; I kept away from him; I avoided him; I lived but for my child. Then, when the end came, and I had to stand by and see it die—die because the help extended to many other children was withheld from it; then I saw that I had made it my idol, and that in every particular I had failed towards the man I had vowed to...."

"But how could you when he was mad?" asked Grace; "it was quite impossible."

"I also said that to myself, Grace, but I knew that when I stood beside him and took those terrible vows—vows I never realised till I heard them slowly and solemnly pronounced before God's altar—Oh, Grace, you are very dear to me, but, when you talk of my sacrifice being thrown away, I think of my child's life sacrificed. Oh, Grace, can you not see that I sinned? What could I expect? How is it that girls so thoughtlessly take those awful things upon themselves, say those words, and yet do not mean them: and yet I did it!"

"But you did it for me, darling—for me—and it does seem different. You did not do it for yourself."

"God knows I did not," said poor Margaret, upon whose fragile and delicate frame this scene was acting feverishly. "But I did it. We need not argue about it, dear; we need not discuss it any more, we should never think of it alike! We are different, dear, and we see things differently—very very differently."

"Then you have quite—quite made up your mind to remain poor all your life, and to let these things slip away from you?" asked Grace, in a tragical tone.

"I will not use that money," said Margaret firmly, "either for you or myself."

"It is too hard," and Grace again dissolved in tears.

Margaret sat down again. She was not yet very strong, and she felt all this cruelly. She let Grace alone for a few moments, then she said—

"If I knew exactly what you wanted, Grace, I might see if it could not be done in another way."

Her voice was cold, with all her tenderness and kindness. She was deeply wounded by her sister's utter inability to understand something of the past.

"Now you are angry, Margaret, and it is a little unreasonable of you. Because you have done with your life, and cannot think about pleasant things any more, why may I not look forward?"

Margaret started. Had she done with her life? She was not yet twenty; was everything really over for her? As regarded marriage or love, of course there was an end; but in her own way she meant to fill her life with happiness, even though a cloud of regret must ever dim its brightness. Her whole being craved for something to give her a full life—interest in some one thing. All the poetical side of her nature began once more to thrill her. The world had much that was sad in it, but there were yet depths unsounded of which she was vaguely aware, and till she knew them she would not proclaim all was over for her even here. The glow of returning health, the beauty of the noontide of summer, began to assert influences she could not totally disregard. As love invests the most homely personal attributes with indefinite charm, so poetry, in its highest, widest, and largest sense, throws a halo over the common-place phases of existence, touches everything with a golden light, and makes it beautiful.

Nothing was more curious than the swift thoughts which carried the one sister above and beyond the present, and the concentration of the other upon a matter so essentially mundane as a brown velvet dress, for Grace counted it as one of her claims to merit that she had tenacity of purpose—which tenacity, if applied to higher purposes, might have deserved commendation.

She watched Margaret's countenance eagerly, and brought her down to worldly matters very soon by her anxiety to know how Margaret proposed arranging matters.

"What do you think of doing?" she asked, eagerly; "and, if you are going to arrange matters, can you not arrange about my clothes also?"

She leaned forward as she spoke, and watched her sister's face intently.

"Grace, it is very foolish of me to forget that you and I have always thought differently about dress and other things. Of course, if I do manage to carry out my plan, you must have clothes and things; if I can arrange it all I will arrange it quite comfortably for you; but you must be patient, dear."

"I hate the conditional tense," said Grace, and then, as she brightened a little, she said, cheerfully—"I believe you will manage it, and you are really a great darling."

"There is one thing more, one caution I want to give you, Grace. Will you be careful about your health? You are marvellously well just now, but you know yourself, dear, how delicate you are. If you do not take care you will be in a sick room again."

"Oh! please don't croak and be horrid now you are just beginning to be nicer again."

"Poor Grace!" said Margaret, with a little sigh.

She went to her own room, and, drawing her chair near the window, sat down to think over the plan she had made. She was resolved to be indebted to no one. If her sister went to London the necessary money should come from no one but herself.

She opened her despatch-box, and looked through her papers. She wanted to find the address of the publisher who had expressed his appreciation of her writing in so substantial a manner.

She looked in vain. She could find it nowhere. Then she recollected that Sir Albert Gerald had carried out all the arrangements for her, and that she had corresponded through him.

She had no hesitation in writing to him since he was a friend now and only a friend. The tragedy of her child's death had blotted out the remembrance of what had been, and she had passed through so much trial, she was so much changed, that she never for one moment doubted but that the change would be equal as regarded him. Her letter was direct, simple, and free from all allusion to her sorrow. She said she wanted to be put into direct communication with the friendly publisher—then she added, "I want to make some money. This may surprise you, as I believe I am supposed to be very rich, but I think you will understand that money must come in an acceptable way or be rejected. I do not intend using the money which has been left me for myself, and I want, if possible, to owe it to no one but myself."

Then she waited patiently.

In her letters to Mrs. Dorriman she wrote fully about her own plans. "I wish to start certain things, to see and judge for myself, and to use the money, which has come to me, for helping little children and others. When I have arranged everything, may I come to you and Uncle Sandford. I shall not be very poor because I believe I have it in my power to make money. I have already done so, but Grace cannot go to Scotland. As soon as I can arrange it for her, she is going to London to stay there with some one, at any rate, for a time."

Mrs. Dorriman read this letter with the most intense satisfaction.

Margaret had grown very dear to her, and in her letter she gave Mr. Sandford the name he had always wished to hear from her. The fact of her offering to come back must show him how completely she had forgiven him.

Ever since that marvellous revelation about Inchbrae, Mrs. Dorriman's manner to her brother had been both tender and affectionate. She tried to prove that her forgiveness was complete, and she could not understand why, now this burden was off his mind, he still made allusion to a weight there.

Often when he came in and she rose to greet him she caught him watching her as though something was still between them, and that helpless feeling of not being able fully to understand pressed upon her again.

He came in one day, looking tired, and she saw that he sank wearily into his chair.

Tea was there, and she gave him some, and made one of those trivial remarks people are apt to make when wandering thoughts are the order of the day.

"Anne, I do not think Margaret will care to come here," he said suddenly, "and you think so too."

Mrs. Dorriman's delicate face flushed a little. "Margaret offers to come," she said after a little pause.

"I find business tires me more and more," he said, as it seemed to her, irrelevantly.

"I am sorry," she answered, looking a little anxiously in his direction.

"Why should we not all go to your house," he asked, as though putting the plainest and simplest question in the world.

"To Inchbrae! Oh, brother!" This sudden suggestion filled her with such intense happiness that she could get no further.

"I want Margaret to get well and I mean to resign my chairmanship and other things. I shall give up business. I want—rest."

His manner alarmed her, but she tried to compose herself, and to accept this new turn in her affairs quietly, and not to let him see how intensely this affected her.

She subdued her emotion and spoke in a matter-of-fact tone, "It will be a long journey for Margaret and for poor Jean."

"I have thought of that. When Margaret refused to accept the arrangement Drayton had made for her, I heard from Stevens, and have been in correspondence with him ever since. I think he might bring her here; there are a great many things to arrange."

"But if we go to Inchbrae, brother, might she not come there, direct?"

"Yes, you may go there and receive her. I must see Stevens here;" and then he continued in a strange tone, "if you wish me to follow you I will go there."

"If I wish it?"

"You do not know, Anne. You know nothing," he exclaimed, with something of his old very peremptory manner.

She was startled and vexed. Why did he go on like this? why constantly talk as if she had yet much to learn?

"One thing more," he said, in a less excited tone, "I do not want every idiot in the place to gossip, and talk, and wonder; go and see the few neighbours with whom you have made acquaintance and speak of going home, and of receiving Margaret naturally. If you leave suddenly no one knows what may be said."

"And about you, brother?"

"About me? who cares?" he said; "my act in the play is nearly over. What does it all matter to me? But you can say I am ill—that is the truth, I am ill."

"If you are ill, I will not leave you."

"Nonsense! my body is well enough, but there is something that hurts far more than bodily illness."

A commotion in the hall was followed by the servant's entrance.

He announced the arrival of a box for Mrs. Dorriman.

She forgot, at the moment, that she had sent to the Macfarlanes for the famous box which held so much that was important to her, and when she saw it it gave her a little shock. Apparently it gave a greater shock to her brother, for he was white to the very lips.

"Anne," he said, and his voice was full of entreaty, "will you do me one great favour: Will you not look at the contents of this box, will you not break the seals, till you are at Inchbrae?"

Mrs. Dorriman—who had seen it arrive with a curiously mingled feeling, half dreading half anxious to know its contents—said quietly, "It shall be as you wish, brother."

CHAPTER IV.

The long July days were at hand, so much longer in the Highlands than in other parts of Great Britain, and which most people, living in that favoured spot, think more than makes up for the shorter winter days. Over everything lay the beauty of summer. Where the heat is not too intense for enjoyment, what a delicious thing is a long, summer day!

At Inchbrae, where the sea kept the air cool, it was perfect; by the side of the burn and down by the waterfall, ferns sprinkled with spray, showed a perpetual verdure, a thousand flowers lingered within the freshness of the burn-side; honeysuckle and sweetbriar rivalled each other in fragrance.

The garden near the house was in perfection, for, though spring flowers come late, they make up for it when they arrive—and roses and geraniums made bright colour, and caught the sunshine to enhance their beauty.

Mrs. Dorriman had felt much on arriving at the little place where she had gone through so much sorrow. Inchbrae, to her, was second to the old home, where she had many memories, but she loved it, and it was her very own, and the fact of possession gives a certain touch of pride in everything.

Christie had welcomed her with all the heartiness of an old Highland friend and dependent. She had scrubbed and cleaned, and Mrs. Dorriman, while missing Jean at every turn, was full of gratitude.

"Eh, my dear, time has stood still for you," Christie said to her, as she watched her quick movements to and fro; "you are a different woman to what you were when you went away."

"I am happier, Christie."

"Aye, you are happier, but you have to get more yet; there's more good to come to you yet."

Mrs. Dorriman laughed softly.

"Are you prophesying a husband to me at my age, and another husband too?" and then she blamed herself for laughing.

"Your age is no hindrance; but I was not thinking of marrying; I was thinking of the old house, of the old home."

"Oh, don't," said Mrs. Dorriman, raising her hands as though pushing the thought from her; "do not make me unhappy by making me think of that. The old place is sold, Christie, and gone from us, gone from me, and I mean to be happy here."

"It will come back to you," Christie said, persistently; "you will see that it will be yours again some day, and it's not a far-off day, either," she added, more to herself than to Mrs. Dorriman.

Mrs. Dorriman turned away. At that moment, with the broad sea rippling and sparkling beneath, taking a thousand hues as it reflected the moving clouds, and the sea-breeze coming upon her with its exquisite freshness, she felt horribly ungrateful for giving a lingering thought to that other home.

But here, with all its beauty, there was a charm lacking—the charm of memory.

Inchbrae had no associations for her, and in that other home there was the dear, kind face of the father, who would doubtless have done more for her had he only had it in his power.

She stood silently trying to stifle any regrets, and to be thankful and grateful for this, the little home she had to offer Margaret.

Margaret had done a good deal, but not all she had hoped to do. She had seen sights that had made her heart sore, and she had helped in many ways, following lines already laid down, and enabling many charities to extend their action. Children learned to watch for her, and those standing round marvelled at the tenderness and skill of her way of handling them.

Knowing her to be childless they were surprised.

Margaret seldom spoke of her little one now. Deep down in her heart she cherished its memory—for a true mother never forgets—but she could not open the wound to strangers or explain why a sick child commanded her strongest compassion.

Her own name was never brought forward, and all the money arrangements were made for her by Mr. Stevens.

She found the other plan she wished to carry out with regard to Grace much more difficult.

Lady Lyons had spoken the truth as regarded finding the "great lady," with whom alone Grace imagined she would find perfect happiness, and be "in the swim." She could hear of no one who had the slightest ambition to chaperone a young lady who was not very beautiful, not very rich, and nobody in particular. Grace had more than one interview with what she called hopeful people; and she was too fond of a joke, even against herself, not to repeat them, and even act the scenes, for Margaret's benefit.

But the plain fact remained that she could hear of nothing the least like what she wanted; and Grace, at no time a miracle of patience, got extremely irritable, and accused the world in general of combining together to defeat her.

Margaret, coming home full of the terrible scenes to which she could not accustom herself, was worried beyond description. The sharp contrast between this unfulfilled longing on the part of her sister for mere amusement, and the terrible—sometimes horrible—realities, to which she had just before perhaps been standing face to face, struck her painfully. She was but human herself, and there arose between them sometimes angry words and sharp retorts that filled her with dismay afterwards.

In characters so widely apart as theirs, it was only to be expected that a day would come when some tremendous crisis would show each how strained the sisterly chords now were.

After a scene between them, however, it was Margaret who tried to make amends for a recognised deficiency in her affection, by giving Grace something she wished for.

At this moment, with that curious disregard to the fitness of things which distinguishes some people, Lady Lyons made a successful effort to see Margaret—with a purpose.

As we know, poor Lady Lyons was one of those mothers who possess no real knowledge of their sons' characters, and she fancied that Paul (who never accused himself of it) was probably too shy to say a few necessary words to show Margaret that, when time had made things a little pleasanter for everybody, he hoped to find her able to respond to his devotion.

She thought that now movement was in the air, and Margaret was talking of going to Scotland, it would considerably help matters if she could say some little thing to arouse Margaret's attention, and to let her see that though Paul kept away (out of delicacy) he was hovering, so to speak, upon the horizon.

Lady Lyons therefore arrived upon the scene one day, and came into the drawing-room, to find Margaret much perturbed and Grace crying upon a sofa.

This was very interesting. Had the sisters been indulging in plain speaking, a matter in which the best of sisters occasionally show more of the licence of their relationship, than of the bond of union supposed to exist between them?

She was always distinctly maternal towards Margaret, hoping she understood, while a little disappointed that Margaret never sufficiently unbent to enable her to embrace her.

Margaret, when in good spirits, was inclined to make fun of her to Grace as rather "a gushing old lady," and the intended maternal impression was, so far, unsuccessful.

Before Lady Lyons had arranged her ideas entirely, Grace, much to her sister's surprise, took Lady Lyons into their counsel, and spoke openly to her of her hopes, her disappointments, and all else, and ended by saying—

"You were quite right, Lady Lyons—no one will have anything to say to me."

"My dear Miss Rivers," said the mistaken woman, and speaking in a most patronising tone, "Don't be afraid, your day will come. You will see, your day will come."

"You are all wrong," said Grace, very much annoyed with her; "I am talking of a chaperone."

"Grace, there is really no use in troubling Lady Lyons with our private affairs," said Margaret, in a tone she trusted would check Grace's indiscretion.

"Nonsense!" said Grace, coolly. "Now, Lady Lyons, here is the whole thing. I want to go and have a little peep at London" (Grace's ideas had become a little modified); "I do not expect to go to royal garden-parties, and all those very swell things, but I want to go to balls and do pleasant things. I am pining to have some fun."

"I am sure it is very natural," said Lady Lyons, a little touched by these girlish sentiments.

"Margaret does not agree with you," said Grace. "She is quite happy spending her time in hospitals and very gruesome places, where she looks after sick people—that is *her* idea of happiness. It is not mine."

"But, my dear Miss Rivers, a very wealthy person has every right to have *some* whims, and dear Mrs. Drayton may perhaps come round after a bit," said Lady Lyons, nodding her head at Margaret with effusiveness.

"You don't understand her," said Grace, who would not stop her confidences—because she wanted to tease her sister—"you call her rich, but she is not at all rich. She has given away all her money, Lady Lyons; she has sent thousands here, there, and everywhere. She will not touch it. I call it a horrid shame!" and Grace buried her face in her handkerchief.

To say that Lady Lyons was speechless is to say very little. She had the most extraordinary feeling, as though in some way Paul had been defrauded.

"It is the most extraordinary thing I ever heard in my life!"

Margaret rose and held out her hand, and wished her good-bye.

"There is no reason it should not be known," she said, with a heightened colour, "though I think my sister might have told the story differently."

Lady Lyons shook hands with her, and the change in her manner would have been most amusing had any one been there to see it.

When Margaret had left the room a sudden idea came to the excellent woman she had left sitting there. She moved a little nearer to Grace and said emphatically,

"Tell me, my dear Miss Rivers, now do be frank with me. How did that dear, good Mr. Sandford take your sister's marriage? Was he angry?"

"He was furious," answered Grace. "It was very ridiculous of him, as he brought the horrible man to the house in the first place, so he is the very last person who ought to find fault."

"And, when Mrs. Drayton goes to Scotland, she does not mean going to stay with Mr. Sandford?"

"Of course not. In that case I shall not be able to go to her eventually."

"And it really was a great deal of money that she has given up."

"It was thousands," said Grace, "and I must say, Lady Lyons, I think it was very selfish, she might have thought of *me*."

"I think she might indeed."

"Because she does not care for money that is no reason why I do not. I *hate* poverty."

"Most people do, it seems a very great pity," said Lady Lyons, feelingly, with a sigh.

"I do not pretend to be like Margaret, I do care for pretty things. I think I *love* clothes," said Grace, reflectively; "and, what is more, I never intend marrying any one who is not as rich as rich can be!"

"I think you are quite right, my dear, quite right, and having no money of your own."

"But I have plenty of money of my own," and Grace opened her eyes very wide, "I mean I have as much as I want from Mr. Sandford, but I should like to be extravagant."

"Excuse me, my dear Miss Rivers, pray excuse me, but you are a little inconsistent, you say you have money, plenty of money, and then you are angry because your sister gives hers away."

"I have plenty for a girl, that is, Margaret gives me everything I want, but I should like to have a house in London, horses, carriages, to be able to throw away money, to feel really *rich*! Now Margaret always puts such a disagreeable question to me. When I say I want something, she says 'Can you do without it?' Why one never would buy decent clothes if one said *that*," and Grace gave a very heavy sigh.

"Supposing, my dear Miss Rivers, only supposing, that you found a lady willing to be your chaperone, what share in the household expenses would you take?" Lady Lyons fixed her eyes with great eagerness on the girl's face.

"None!" said Grace, calmly.

Lady Lyons started.

"But if a lady went to London and took a house, and got carriages and servants, all on your account, she would expect you to share expenses."

"Then she would be quite wrong, and I have no idea of going to London with any one who knows nobody, who has not made even a beginning. For instance," and Grace spoke laughingly, "supposing you yourself thought of such a thing, why there would be no use; I daresay you know a few people, but all your acquaintances are very likely ... fossils," and Grace burst into a hearty fit of laughter. Lady Lyons drew her cloak round her and put on her most dignified manner.

"I will wish you good morning, Miss Rivers; of course my health alone would prevent my ever thinking of undertaking such a charge!"

"Now you are offended with me, Lady Lyons. Of course I was wrong to say fossils, but the word somehow slipped out. I do beg your pardon—you know I am a dreadful goose—do forgive me!"

Lady Lyons was not very easily appeased. She was naturally very irate at the word used, and she was deeply offended also at having been in a way rejected before she had proposed anything, but she wished to think over this idea of Grace Rivers. She had always had a hankering for London doctors, feeling vaguely that in some wonderful way health and strength and even youth might be renewed by their united skill.

Though Grace had so decidedly put her upon one side, she knew that this was not final. She was shrewd enough to see that if the girl could not carry out her plan in any other way she might be asked to undertake the task; and, though she was an invalid, so much of her ailment was on her nerves, that cheerful society might do her good.

She extended the hand of forgiveness to Grace, therefore, with a tinge of patronage, and peace was so far established between them.

Much to Margaret's indignation Grace insisted upon advertising, and her advertisement caused no little discussion between the sisters.

"I shall put it, 'A young lady of position, and of good birth, wishes to reside with a lady of ...' I am afraid if I put in 'rank' it will look snobbish," she said, reflectively, "and I do not care if she has rank or not. I only want to be with somebody who knows every one!"

"I do not see how you can word it so as to express your whole meaning," said Margaret; "and you really do not know, yourself, what you want."

Grace smiled.

"Oh, yes, I do. I want plenty of really good society. Why go over it all again?"

"Because you are asking what I fancy is an impossibility. If you were an heiress, then all would be easy enough; but with moderate means, I repeat, no one with a position will be troubled with such a charge."

Grace however persisted, and when the advertisement had been for some days staring her in the face she received two answers.

"Lady Turnbull will be glad to afford an interview to the young lady wishing to go into society, and wishes to know what sum the young lady proposes to contribute in return for chaperonage, board, lodging, and anxiety of mind."

"The woman must be mad!" exclaimed Grace. "Anxiety of mind! I never heard anything so ridiculous."

The other letter was from a Mrs. Geoffrey Lansdowne Bill, who used her name in extenso through it, from end to end.

"Mrs. Geoffrey Lansdowne Bill, having rather a more roomy house than she requires, would resign two rooms to the young lady who advertised for a happy and refined home and chaperonage. Mrs. Geoffrey Lansdowne Bill, having married two of her daughters well, would be quite prepared to farther the young lady's views in that direction.

"The society among which she moves is mixed, partaking of the literary and fashionable equally. Mrs. Geoffrey Lansdowne Bill of course expects to be very handsomely remunerated for her trouble, and I wish to hear from the young lady at once."

Even Margaret laughed heartily over this effusion.

"A pity one of her literary friends did not help her to write her letter," she said, laughing, as she looked it over, "and keep her tenses in order."

"I should think the society was 'mixed,'" exclaimed Grace, wrathfully, "and I know what you are thinking—you think that these two failures will prove me to be quite wrong—you imagine that this will convince me that my plan is an impossible one—but I mean to do it somehow."

"Very well," said Margaret, very quietly.

Only two days after this Grace came into the room, with a rush, and announced that Mr. Stevens was there and wished to see her; and, in the same breath, she added, "I have seen Lady Lyons, and she is going to look after me, she has gone to London to see about rooms, and now nothing remains but for you to say how much money you can give me. I shall want plenty, you know, and do not keep me a moment in suspense." Before Margaret could answer her she was gone.

There was always a bitter sense of humiliation to poor Margaret when the question of her husband's money had to be touched upon.

She had seldom seen Mr. Stevens, though they had a great deal of correspondence. He never could understand her views. Having married Mr. Drayton for his money in the first instance, why did she refuse to benefit by his will afterwards?

This apparent inconsistency troubled him; he had judged her harshly before they had met, and now he had learned to like her so well that he wanted some explanation of her conduct that would satisfy him.

He came to see her, now, because some things had remained unexplained, and he felt that much trouble and correspondence might be saved by a personal interview.

Margaret never saw him without emotion. She had that sort of instinct, we most of us have, about the liking or disliking an acquaintance has for us, and she knew that, though he showed her civility and even compassion, she had not his approval.

How could he approve of her, knowing only the bare fact of her marriage? Sometimes she longed to tell him at any rate so much as might set her right in his eyes, because the disapprobation of an essentially just man was painful to her.

But the circumstances that had led to her marriage, and which she had judged to be so important at the time, had been proved to possess no real importance. She had yielded to her sister's weak dread of a poverty she detested, and her hope of escaping to a more congenial atmosphere; and, when she found that Margaret's sacrifice had not altered her conditions, she calmly accepted them as the inevitable, and poor Margaret felt that all she had suffered had not been in reality demanded of her.

In this lay the sting of it all—and she could not now bring herself back to that excitement of feeling and agony of mind about Grace which had pushed her into an action she now so bitterly regretted.

"You have resigned all Mr. Drayton's money now, Mrs. Drayton," said Mr. Stevens, after a long conversation. "This last cheque to the Children's Hospital is the last balance, as far as regards you. Of course your sister's remains untouched, and, I suppose, as the investment is a good one, she will not care to disturb it."

"My sister's?" inquired Margaret, wonderingly. "What money do you refer to?"

"Do you not remember? Mr. Drayton told me you made a great point of it—that you asked him to settle something on her—that in the event of his death she should be provided for."

Margaret did remember it now with a hot blush of shame. Yes, it had been part of her bargain.

"How much is there?" she asked in a low voice.

Mr. Stevens looked at her in surprise.

"There are fifteen thousand pounds; the life interest is left to you only; the money becomes hers at your death. You see, therefore, you cannot alienate this sum. You cannot give it away."

"I am sure my sister will think with me...." she began, and then stopped suddenly; she had a conviction that Grace would think very differently.

"I do not know if you can enter into my feeling about Mr. Drayton's money," she said, hurriedly. "It is no whim, no distaste for the comforts and luxuries of life, but I cannot!" she continued, with a tone of passion surprising to him in one usually so quiet and impassive before him. A great sob broke her voice. She felt ashamed of betraying emotion before one she conceived to be unsympathetic, and in a moment or two she checked all signs of it, and said in a calmer tone: "I trust my sister will see all this as I do."

"I do not think she will," said Mr. Stevens, who felt intensely for her, and who liked her better than he had ever thought possible. "But I do not think that her action in the matter need disturb you, people are so differently constituted. I myself fully appreciate your feeling in the matter; it is honourable to you, if you will allow me to say so."

"I am so glad you understand," said Margaret, simply. "I have been afraid that you could not approve...."

She stopped short, afraid of again breaking down; and then, in a calmer voice, turned to the subject of those scenes she had so lately visited, and the wants of the poor children she was so interested in.

He was more and more charmed with her; here was no high-flown nonsense, no exaggerated sentiment, but all her schemes were practical and full of common sense.

He stayed long, then he said,

"The only thing to be settled now is, whether the interest from the fifteen thousand pounds you will have nothing to do with is to be applied to charitable purposes or paid to your sister?"

"I will write to you."

"Do; and Mrs. Dorriman, do you know, is trusting to me to see you safe through the perils of your long journey."

"But it will give you so much trouble."

"Not at all;" he spoke in such a kind tone that Margaret felt she had gained him as a friend.

"Dear Mrs. Dorriman," she said softly, "what a lesson she is to us all; so unselfish and so perfectly unconscious of all her own virtues!"

He was silent, and after a few moments he left her and she waited for Grace, full of a certain vague unrest, not knowing what she would do, more than half afraid that she would see nothing but satisfaction in the fact of having an income, unable to sympathise with the difference that lay between them, forgetting that Grace knew, after all, very little of those dreadful months, and that it was quite impossible for her to see things from her point of view.

She turned to pleasanter things. Lying on the table was a small parcel. She well knew what it was, as she had a letter from the publisher that morning.

The proofs of her poem lay before her. Though she had concealed her name her first idea was one almost of fear. She had poured out her whole heart in these lines—her sorrows, her bitter mourning over the past. Reading it all now, how vividly it all came back to her! The lines on her child's death touched her with fresh sorrow; again she felt the terribly blank feeling of loss, and stretched once more her empty arms towards an unanswering grave.

It was into this wave of feeling that Grace's voice broke, and it jarred upon her even more than usual.

With a hurried knock, as though a formality she might dispense with, and without waiting for an answer, Grace came in, all her clothes and her light fluffy hair in a state of discomposure.

"Margaret!" she exclaimed, "I am going away; either I leave the house or Jean—that most tiresome, provoking, aggravating, old Scotchwoman. I will not stay here if she remains!"

"What in the world has happened now?" said poor Margaret, worried and troubled, and speaking with a certain sharpness not habitual to her.

"You need not speak to me like that. Of course you will take her part; but she has been so impertinent I will not stand it!"

"I ask you again," said Margaret, "what has she done? She nursed you faithfully and most kindly. What offence has she given you now?"

"She called me a Jezebel, and then said I had a leg in the grave."

"I doubt her saying this, and—oh, Grace, how can you?" and Margaret got up and looked steadily at her sister, her own face flushing red as she spoke.

"It is nothing to make a fuss about," said Grace, trying to laugh it off, "and it is you yourself who are to blame; you do not know how trying it is to hear you say one day I am looking very pale and am I well, and another day something of the same kind. I will not be ill, Margaret, do you hear?"

"I hear," said poor Margaret, in a low voice, shocked and distressed. To her primitive ideas the fact of Grace using rouge was a degradation she could not get over.

"You are as bad as Jean," said Grace, angrily: "and I have been waiting for that tiresome man to be gone to tell you my plans. What in the world had he to talk about to-day?"

"His business referred more to you than to me," and Margaret, still annoyed and ruffled, spoke very coldly.

Grace was in one of her most provoking moods; she was trying to hide any discomposure she felt by an air of bravado, and she resented Margaret's sharpness as though her sister was injuring her deeply by her tone.

"Did he come to offer me his hand?" she asked, drawing herself up and looking at Margaret with raised eyebrows; "perhaps, middle-aged as he is, he may think as one sister——Oh, forgive me, darling Margaret! I am hateful and detestable! No one but you would have patience with me! I will go and ask Jean's pardon! I will do anything only don't look so!"

She flung herself upon her knees by Margaret, weeping passionately.

"Grace, there are only we two; let us love each other, and not drift into unkindness," whispered Margaret, and Grace checked her weeping and got up.

"Now tell me," she said, "what you mean, darling. In what way did his visit refer to me?"

"Mr. Drayton, it seems, to please me," began Margaret.... "No," she said, "I must put it to *you* truthfully. When I agreed to marry him I stipulated that out of his wealth he should provide for you in such a way that if I died or he died you should be beyond want."

"And what did he do?" asked Grace, breathlessly, her eyes sparkling with eagerness.

"He left fifteen thousand pounds to you and the life interest to me, Grace."

"And he left nothing to me outright! What a shame!" and Grace's eyes filled with angry tears.

"He knew that so long as I lived you would share anything I had," said Margaret, gently.

"Which it seems is little enough, as you are reducing yourself to a state of pauperism by degrees," said Grace, bitterly.

"You have all you want, and Mr. Sandford's liberal allowance is more than sufficient for us both."

"And as I do not wish you to die, darling, and you are stronger than I am, it is a very empty compliment."

"I do not wish to touch this money, Grace. I hope you will not touch it either."

"How can I touch it if it is yours?"

"But if I do not take the income it will either accumulate for you or I believe you could have the interest now."

"Delightful!" exclaimed Grace. "Now, Margaret, you may spare yourself any remarks. I have this money within my reach and I intend to take it,—there!"

CHAPTER V.

If Margaret had continued to have any hopes of her sister's seeing matters as she saw them she would soon have been undeceived. Grace's spirits were a real trial to her, but this was nothing compared to the congratulations that poured in from Lady Lyons, and even from Jean.

Grace announced to every one that she had succeeded to a fortune, and made no secret of its having been a legacy from her brother-in-law.

If any thing could have added to Margaret's feeling about it, it was being congratulated upon her husband's having done the right thing.

Lady Lyons was quite bewildered by Grace's impetuous confidences—though with all her questioning she could not make out exactly what the fortune was. Grace's expression 'heaps of money' might mean any thing.

How tiresome it was that she had definitely refused her chaperonage! How stupidly she had acted—it was really very provoking that sometimes people could not look forward and see more clearly what lay behind the veil of futurity.

Just as she was extremely provoked with herself, Margaret, for the first time since her trouble, came to see her.

She looked very fair and sweet in the plain black dress she wore, and Lady Lyons, who was kind-hearted, was touched by the signs of sorrow so easily read in her countenance, and received her with a momentary forgetfulness of her own position as an invalid.

Margaret knew nothing of what had passed between her sister and Lady Lyons, and she had come because she was really anxious to arrange something soon. She was urged by Mrs. Dorriman to hurry north that she might have the heat of the summer by the sea, and she could not go till her sister was safely placed with some one in whom she had some confidence.

Before Lady Lyons could arrange her ideas, and say what she wished about the legacy, Margaret had asked her point-blank if she would undertake the charge of Grace.

Lady Lyons was flattered and pleased, and, for a moment or two, did nothing but talk incoherently about the compliment.

"I do not think you need consider it a great compliment," said Margaret, smiling, "unless you feel that my good opinion is one. It is best to be frank, Lady Lyons; my sister is not strong, she is not equal to all she wishes to do, and I shall be much happier leaving her under your care than with a stranger."

"I am not a stranger, certainly, and I have friends, but I am not certain they will please your sister. I am not fashionable, and I do not know fashionable people."

"I do not think Grace will mind that," said Margaret, innocently.

Lady Lyons looked at her rather curiously. "You and your sister are not at all like each other, Mrs. Drayton; when she spoke to me she distinctly gave me to understand I was not good enough and did not know any but fossils. Yes, that was the word, *fossils*!"

There was an offended tone—it was evident she had not forgiven Grace yet.

"Grace talks nonsense sometimes, Lady Lyons; you can afford to laugh at these things. I did not know she had already asked you to take her to London, or I should not have troubled you."

"Oh! she did not ask me; we put a supposititious case to each other," said Lady Lyons, afraid now that things might still not come to a happy conclusion. "Frankly, dear Mrs. Drayton, I should, myself, like to go to London for a while. I often feel one of those good London doctors would set me up after a bit. I have often wished to be nearer them. Now, from here, by the time I get to the station, and then get to their houses, and then back again, I am quite worn out, and then there is the expense."

"Yes, there is the expense." Margaret spoke a little dreamily; she could not help thinking that if Lady Lyons spent her time running after doctors Grace would hardly have what she bargained for.

"Of course, Mrs. Drayton, expense is nothing to you who throw away thousands," said Lady Lyons in an injured tone.

"Do I throw away thousands?" asked Margaret, who did not know how busy rumour had been as regarded her fortune and what she had done with it. "I think not, but I was wondering, perhaps, if the charge of a young girl like my sister was not too much for you."

"Oh, no!" exclaimed Lady Lyons, afraid of seeing all her visions fade away. "I only meant that I might at first see some one, and be put in a right way."

"Grace will want to go everywhere, to all the plays, and concerts, and every attainable thing," said Margaret, impressively. "You must not accept the position with your eyes shut."

"I assure you, dear Mrs. Drayton, I do understand it all, a young girl, and never having had any pleasure. I only mentioned about doctors, because it is, you know, one of the advantages of London—you can get, as a learned friend of mine once said, the best advice for your soul and body."

This conversation did not impress Margaret very favourably, but time was running on, and she had given up her house. With all Lady Lyons' nonsense and absurdity she was a kind-hearted woman, and no one would ever have any real influence with Grace.

That young lady took it all very calmly. She did not object to Lady Lyons, or evince any surprise at her being ready now to do what she had proclaimed herself reluctant to do before; but she was so completely absorbed by the approaching change in her existence that Margaret was hurt to find how little she seemed to feel the separation from herself.

The sisters parted. Margaret gave her last look, and saw Grace in the celebrated brown velvet, which, in a warm June day, was singularly inappropriate, looking fragile but radiant, ordering about the porters, and quite giving herself the airs of a young person of consequence.

With a sigh, Margaret leaned back; this one close tie did not bring her much satisfaction.

As the train swept on through the rich country, however, the new expectation, the movement, and change of scene, wrought their own work. The soft colour came into her face. For the first time she found herself looking forward instead of looking back.

Everything was pleasant to her that day. She was alone, Jean having sturdily refused to share her carriage, and she had nothing to disturb her. Never had she seen the foliage richer, she thought, and she looked at the myriads of cowslips and ox-eyed daisies with a sudden longing to be near them. She had a book with her, but she never opened it. She had had a great pleasure, in a most friendly letter from her publisher—with a substantial proof of his admiration for her book of poems, and asking for the names of those she wished to send them to.

Margaret smiled over this request. She had not a friend in the world she cared to tell about her writing. Yes! one friend, Sir Albert Gerald, and to him she would send her little book and write. He had been so kind, and he was very good.

She was roused from these reflections by the entrance of Mr. Stevens into the carriage. He had been in a smoking-carriage part of the way, and he now came in, bringing various papers to while away the tedium of the journey.

His entrance broke up her reverie. She had grown to like him, though she sometimes thought how much finer a character his would be if he could only put suspicion more on one side. His first impulse was to doubt everything and everybody; and his caution was carried to such an extreme that his friendships were few, and only extended after a long period of probation.

The train stopped at York, and Margaret, under his escort, went to get some refreshment.

As she was returning to her carriage she heard her name uttered in surprise, and in another moment Sir Albert Gerald himself stood beside her.

She was unfeignedly glad to see him, and they plunged into quite an animated conversation, forgetting for the moment everything save that accident had brought them once more together.

Margaret was first recalled to the present by Mr. Stevens, who reminded her that the train would go on without her if she did not hurry. Even then she turned naturally to Sir Albert, and he hurried along with her; and, to Mr. Stevens's great dissatisfaction, got in and calmly sat down opposite to her.

Why the older man took exception to this no one can say; but his suspicions were all on the alert, and everything the young man did seemed to him significant.

Margaret, of course, introduced them to each other, explaining, as Mr. Stevens thought, in a manner utterly unnecessary, that he was travelling down to Scotland to take care of her. But the brief words seemed only an interruption to the flow of talk. At first they both tried to bring him into the conversation, but in vain. He sat grimly in a corner, determined not to be won over by a good-looking young fellow of whom he knew nothing, and wondering at Margaret's glow of colour and animation. Once he heard a little laugh, and he looked up surprised he could make nothing of their conversation. Some one had written a book of poetry—but what could there be said about such nonsense? Any sane man who had something to say could surely say it in good honest prose.

"Do you like poetry," asked Sir Albert, suddenly turning to him pleasantly.

"No, I don't," Mr. Stevens answered with quite unnecessary shortness. "I never see the use of it."

"If useful things only were given to us here," said Margaret, gently, "our lives would be very dull."

"I have no poetry in my life, and I do not feel dull," he answered in a softer manner to her.

"Are you sure you have no poetry in your life?" asked Sir Albert, pleasantly—he was anxious to make friends with a man Margaret liked and respected.

"It is difficult to say where it comes into my life," said Mr. Stevens, more politely, melting a little under the influence of so pleasant a voice and manner. "I am manager in a manufactory, and work is the order of the day.

Till we leave off and I go out home I never breathe the fresh air or see the sun shine."

"But they greet you, then," said Sir Albert, earnestly; "the play of the sunshine upon the river, the ripple of the brook, the endless stories found in every leaf and blossom, the song of the birds, all these sweet gifts are nature's poems given to make us better and wiser men, and happier ones too," he added in a lower voice.

"Put in that way," began Mr. Stevens; and then, a little ashamed of being influenced so soon by a man he had never seen before, he said more abruptly, "I think bringing sentiment into work is the ruin of every thing—what do we want with it? If we use our faculties, and work to the best of our ability, I conceive that is all that is expected of us. I think life is an easy enough problem, though philosophers try and make it out otherwise. We are given two paths, a right one and a wrong one; the right one is often difficult, the wrong one frequently pleasant; it is our own fault if we choose it, and it leads us to disaster."

"*If we use our faculties*," repeated Margaret, in her gentle voice, with a certain emphasis on the words. "Do we use our faculties, Mr. Stevens, if we shut our eyes (that are given to us to make use of) and do not observe what is lovely and fair around us?"

Mr. Stevens was a little staggered by this question. "Looking at flowers and mountains and listening to birds singing, is not poetry," he said, obstinately.

"But if we read a poem and appreciate it, if we listen to music, if we see a fine painting, in short, if we see the poetry in other people's work, it has a good influence on our minds." Sir Albert spoke earnestly.

"I don't see that at all. Working people have no time for poetry and pretty things. Their lives are very different."

"You are indeed mistaken. Much of the misery and the vice amongst the very poorest people are caused by the squalor and absence of any charm or higher influence in their lives. This is so well recognised that many people are spending time and money in trying to improve the look of things for the poor. Think, Mr. Stevens," said Margaret, earnestly, "only think what it must be for a hard-working man to go home to a wretched, comfortless room, without paper on the walls, or an atom of *home*-look about the place, a tired-out wife, and children cross because their natural energies have no outlet. If he could go home to a comfortable room with cheerful colour about it and find it clean. If the children, instead of having access only to the grimy streets, could play in the squares and gardens, so selfishly shut up from them now, their lives would be better, they would take heart, and not find the one relief, the public-house afterwards."

"And a nice sight the squares and gardens would be, in a very short time," Mr. Stevens said, a little moved by Margaret's extreme earnestness, and trying to hide that it affected him.

"Why should they be? Look at the Temple gardens, look at places already open to the public! I would give anything to see all these places thrown open to all."

"And in Paris everything is open, and who shall say we are less well-behaved than the French?" said Sir Albert, backing her up.

"Two against one is hardly fair," said Mr. Stevens, the last shred of prejudice dropping from him, and beginning to find that there was something very delightful in a man who could talk of something besides work.

When after another hour Sir Albert got out of the train Mr. Stevens was quite cordial in expressing his hope that they would meet again at no distant time.

Before they parted, Sir Albert, with a glance at Margaret, promised to send him a book of poetry that would convert him.

"I am going to travel for a year or so," he continued, turning to Margaret, "then I also shall go to Scotland."

She understood what he meant. He was very kind and very thoughtful; but *that* now—that could never be!

When he had left, and the train had started again, she was very much amused to hear Mr. Stevens say—

"There is a great deal to like in that young man. Have you known him long?"

Margaret answered, and told him the story of his most terrible accident.

"And all this happened before your marriage? Most extraordinary!" he said.

Margaret was annoyed with herself, because she felt herself grow crimson.

When he saw her colour he said, with greater emphasis—

"Most extraordinary!"

Both she and Jean were tired enough when they reached Perth. Margaret, indeed, had a certain mental excitement which prevented her sleeping. With the tenderness of conscience, which amounted to something akin to morbidness, she accused herself of having forgotten because she had allowed herself to be happy.

"Alas!" she thought, "is it possible that I am the same miserable broken woman who cared not even for the light of day a few weeks ago? And now a change of scene, meeting with an old friend, has sent courage through my veins, and made life seem sweet to me again."

But there was no use lamenting over feelings which had gone, and she was too honest with herself to blind herself to the fact of being different. Her grief for her child was there sharp and painful, for a mother cannot forget. But the crushing sense of having done something unworthy had been lifted from her. The tone of gentle respect and sympathy shown her by Sir Albert had swept false theories upon one side. She still said to herself, "I have sinned!" but she no longer said, "Heaven can forgive, but man never can!" and the sharpest sting was gone.

Jean was in a state of wild excitement as they drew near the old haunts. Her head was turning in rapid succession from side to side as she recognised the various landmarks.

"Eh!" she exclaimed aloud, greatly to the amusement of the other passengers, "there is the old kirk and the hill behind it, just as I left them."

"You did not expect them to run away, did you?" said an elderly man, watching her keenly.

"I do not know what I expected," she answered, in an abstracted manner, "but they are there—and that is a very great deal to me."

Margaret had no associations, but she also looked eagerly at a place of which she had heard so much.

The great brown hills were sleeping in the sunshine, their beautiful outlines sharp and clear against a pale sky, on which floated a few golden clouds. Between some fir-trees she at length saw the sea.

But it seemed to her that never had she appreciated it so fully before. The purple shadows sweeping over it made the bright radiance of the sun's last rays exquisitely beautiful, and the crest of each restless wave seemed a moving mass of gold. As the train drew up, her eyes were still dazzled by the brilliancy of the picture.

Mrs. Dorriman, inclined to be tearful, and quite resolved not to give way, made singular faces, as she held that forlorn figure to her kindly heart.

"Do not cry, my dear," she said, in a low voice, as she watched Margaret's calm face, expecting every moment to see her break down, and quite astonished at her calmness and self-command.

Margaret was not inclined to cry. The source of her tears lay far too deep. She had wept for her child for months, and still there came that painful spasm if something brought it suddenly before her; but Mrs. Dorriman had no association in connection with it. She reminded her of her girlhood, of

Lornbay, of all that happened there, and any emotion she felt was softened to her now by the soothing influence of Sir Albert Gerald's kindness and sympathy.

"It is like coming home," she said to Mrs. Dorriman.

"My poor child!"

"It is pleasant to feel so at home. I seem to know that bent fir-tree and the look of the hills—and oh! how perfect the air is here!"

"Yes, it is fine," said Mrs. Dorriman, putting her sentiment and tears upon one side as she saw that Margaret needed neither.

"What a delicious scent! What is it?" exclaimed Margaret, as the famous pony-carriage bowled along towards Inchbrae.

"The gorse in full bloom. There is nothing like it," answered the little lady, full of happiness now she had some one who could appreciate all these things at her side. "My own idea is that the breath of the sea and the scent of the gorse-flower and heather would make any one well; and I am so glad, dear—so glad you are here."

"I am glad to be here," said Margaret, thoughtfully; "it is like a beautiful awakening in another and a fairer world after a bad dream."

"And Margaret, love, I do so want to ask you something."

"Ask me anything you like."

"We are not exactly 'kin,' as Jean would say, but would you give me a name? I am too old to be called Anne, but will you not call me something else?"

"I always do. I always think of you as if you were my own, my very own, relation, and do call you 'Auntie.' Will that do?" and Margaret bent and kissed her.

"Oh!" said Mrs. Dorriman with a sigh, "you do not know how sweet it is to have some one to love you. I have had so little affection all my life, and sometimes it makes me feel a little forlorn. I think having a sister must be such an enormous comfort."

"Sometimes," said Margaret, "and sometimes a great anxiety; of course, few ties can come up to it," she added, hastily, afraid of allowing even Mrs. Dorriman to know the intense and bitter disappointment Grace was to her.

They arrived at Inchbrae, and, if Margaret had admired it at all before, she could not help being still more enthusiastic about all now. Can anything in nature excel the charm of a well-kept flower-garden with its gay flower-beds and velvet lawn, and a background of pines with their red stems glowing in the sunset, and a magnificent range of rocks behind it; while through the delicate and graceful birch-trees glimpses of the sea in all its changing beauty and capricious moods is there to give that sense of the Infinite which raises our thoughts above and beyond it all?

Margaret's eyes filled with sudden tears. The loveliness of it all touched and soothed her, and yet she was nearly weeping. She seemed all at once to see that she had hitherto missed something in her life which was now given her. She put up her hand as Mrs. Dorriman was going to speak, and asked, in the lowered tone of one who is conscious of being moved and charmed beyond expression, what the noise was near them?

"It sounds like a river; it is distinct from the solemn thud of the sea I hear breaking on the rocks."

"It is the river; that is the sound I missed so much when I went to Renton," answered Mrs. Dorriman, full of the delight of having Margaret's sympathy.

"It has a rushing mighty sound like the wings of a relentless fate," said Margaret, dreamily; "I never was so near a river before."

"Do you like being so near it? Some people think it disturbs them; that louder noise through all is the waterfall. Come and have some tea now, and, when you are rested, we will go by the river-walk."

"Everything is so lovely," she exclaimed, as she followed Mrs. Dorriman into the bright little drawing-room, and noticed the pretty freshness of everything.

She was delighted with her own room, which was looking towards the sea.

"How you must have felt leaving all this!" she exclaimed as she looked out upon it all.

"I did feel it then, but you soon became my great comfort and pleasure. I am glad I went, for many reasons, but one chief reason is that I learnt to know you there."

Margaret had but one vision of the sea in her memory. She had thought the grand sweep of the bay and the mouth of the Clyde heavenly, and it lingered in her memory as she had watched it with Grace that first night, and had been so entranced with its smooth beauty, upon which the moonlight had thrown such a lovely and silvery veil.

But with all the associations of that place and the vivid remembrance of Sir Albert Gerald's yacht gliding into the bright moonlit streak, like a bird ready to fold her wings and rest,—she felt that there could be no comparison.

No sea, rippling in smoothly, far away from the turbulence and strife, sheltered in the great arms of a bay nearly surrounding it, smiling there even when fierce and angry beyond the shelter, can possibly equal in grandeur the same sea crashing in against perpendicular rocks, dashing itself with terrific strength against an iron-bound coast, as though scorning the obstacles in front of it; and Margaret, her whole heart tender and sensitive to impressions of natural beauty, was carried out of herself by this new scene, so suddenly presented to her.

How small, how little, seemed the former ideas she had had of the place. She was too full of thought to speak much, and her silence suited Mrs. Dorriman, who, while striving to keep every word she said away from subjects likely to touch upon poor Margaret's loss, betrayed by the very pains she took, by her sudden pauses and the hesitation of her manner, that there was an expectation on her side of some emotion she did not wish to arouse.

This would not do.

There were some things in Margaret's life that she could never touch upon with any one. Her husband's madness had been very terrible, so terrible that she never willingly allowed it to remain in her mind, and she never mentioned him.

It was a frightful and crushing trial out of which she had come into the light. Her wings had been scorched and broken in the conflict, but they had not been injured for all time. The stain was not permanent, and she had passed through it all without understanding it, except so far as this, that she believed to every woman an instinct is given as a help. She had wilfully erred against hers, and she had suffered cruelly.

But of her child ... yes, of her child she was longing to speak! the want of sympathy in Grace had sent back all the touching records, so dear to a mother's heart, and she knew that Mrs. Dorriman would give sympathy.

"It is a grief to me," she said, gently, "that you never saw my child. I should like to tell of it, if my speaking of it does not trouble you."

"Oh! my dear," said Mrs. Dorriman, and her voice trembled a little. "Is it wise for you?"

"It is wise," answered Margaret. "I often wish I had a friend near me to whom I could sometimes speak of it—it hurts me to feel that it is not to be mentioned before me, while I feel it still so near me."

Mrs. Dorriman, her anxiety checked about giving Margaret pain, could only answer by a tighter grasp of the arm she clung to.

"Yes, at first it was very dreadful to me. Now at times tears still come, but I am beginning to think of it as waiting for me, not as lying here and leaving me childless and alone. It was very fair, auntie, and had winning ways...." She stopped for a moment and went on in the subdued voice which was her characteristic. "At first I was so selfish and I prayed for death, I, who have still much to do."

"You have seen much illness lately?"

"I have seen many terrible things," she answered, earnestly. "I have seen troubles and trials that dwarf mine; I try to help; it is a great blessing to be able to help. When I stroke the little faded cheek of another child I still think of mine, for I am still selfish in my grief; but the joy of seeing a child recover kills the selfishness, and I begin more to do things for God's sake and theirs, than for the sweet little face always present to me. I am happier since I have learned how to make others happy!"

She paused, folding her hands, and looking to Mrs. Dorriman like some fair saint, with her unclouded eyes and the sweet folded lips that were both grave and tender.

"Here there is poverty, sickness, and often sorrow," said Mrs. Dorriman; "but somehow, with these surroundings, poverty does not seem so grim."

"Here there are springs of water, fresh air and *this*," said Margaret, pointing to the river; "but in London, water is taxed even to the very poor, the very kindling of their fires is a difficulty. Here the people have at any rate kindling," and she added, pointing to a woman in the distance, who was carrying a bundle of furze,

"And peat for the cutting; and yet the ambition of many is to leave the country and flock to the towns."

"The sound of higher wages is tempting, but what I hope to live to see one day is the middle-man done away with."

"The middle-man!" exclaimed Mrs. Dorriman; "I do not understand you, my dear."

"I mean those who pay the manufacturer so little that he often cannot raise wages, or do what he would like to do, and who grasp from the rich as well; and the working class I think of do not understand the question, and not understanding are unjust. They blame the rich, but the rich are not to blame; they pay often a hundred per cent. where the workman does not get ten. It is the middle-man who grows rich grasping on either side, and who spend their money in eating and drinking. They help no art or science, and they are indignant if they are appealed to for charitable aid. You do not know how bad it is!" and Margaret's cheek flushed with her earnest, almost passionate, speech.

"I never thought of it before," said Mrs. Dorriman, "and now I do not quite understand. Shopkeepers have to pay high rents and rates and things."

"Oh, I do not mean the better class of shopkeepers," said Margaret, "and I am talking of small shops I know about in London where coals are sold by the pound and tea in ounces, and those places where shirts are made, literally *made*, for twopence. It is this misery that should be attacked, these things should be made impossible!"

"Why can it not be done?" said Mrs. Dorriman.

"Because ours is such a free country that interference is not often possible. Oh, there is so much to put right it does not bear thinking about," and the two turned up the river-side and home.

CHAPTER VI.

Grace was much too excited to feel keenly the parting with Margaret; indeed, the gravity of her young sister, while, of course, to be accounted for, she felt altogether as a drag upon her energies.

Like other girls of her peculiarly thoughtless nature she hated having to think of anything that was not what she considered cheerful; and she had not the power of throwing herself into the sorrows of any one, even of a sister, whose one fault it was, that she had allowed her clear instincts to be obscured and darkened by her passionate love for Grace, and her wish to give what she thought her very life depended upon at that moment.

Accustomed to be considered, it was new to her to find that she had twice to change her place to suit Lady Lyons, who was one of the women who imagine that, whatever happens to belong to another, from a husband to a corner in a railway-carriage, must be superior to anything they have themselves.

Grace was good-humoured, and changed her seat cheerfully, although she felt the difference. Margaret would have borne any discomfort rather than disturb her. But the thought that she was going to join the world in London and form one of the giddy throng was too enchanting to her not to support her under any surprises—she was so determined to be happy.

She was surprised beyond measure that Margaret's marriage should have left her the winner in the race; but it was satisfactory that, as she cared for money and Margaret did not, she should have it, and Margaret would soon forget that horrible man, who was, however, not all horrible, since he had done this.

"Pray see about your luggage, Miss Rivers," said Lady Lyons, very languidly, when they arrived at the station.

"Surely your maid can do that," said Grace, with a little toss of her head.

"How can she possibly know your luggage when she has never seen it?" asked Lady Lyons, fretfully, but not without a show of reason.

"Maids should have instincts," said Grace, as she sailed along the platform to point out her boxes.

This difficulty overcome they got into a cab, the maid following in another. But, as Lady Lyons was always afraid of being cold, she took a bearskin of some standing, a roll of rugs, and a bottle of lavender-water. She gave the man unnecessarily minute directions, and pulled up her window. It was the last days of a hot June.

Grace let her window down with a bang that very nearly shivered it to atoms.

"My *dear* Miss Rivers, pray put up the window. I have such a languid circulation, and I am ordered by my medical men to be careful about draughts."

"There really cannot be a draught when one window is hermetically closed," said Grace very coolly; "be as stuffy as you like on your side of the carriage, but I must have fresh air."

Lady Lyons was a little daunted, and said nothing. In a moment or two she began to cough, a short cough improvised for the occasion. Grace took no notice.

"If I am very ill you will have to send to Wandsworth for Mr. Jones," she said, at length.

"Why should you be ill? Fresh air is what you want, Lady Lyons. You are coughing on purpose."

"My *dear* Miss Rivers."

"Wait till you hear me cough; then you will know a real cough when you hear one," said Grace laughing and putting up a little bit of window. She did not want to quarrel with Lady Lyons, but she did intend to assert her independence from the first.

They went to a private hotel, where again Grace interfered. She would have nothing but the best rooms, and all the little arrangements put forward in an economical form by poor Lady Lyons were ruthlessly swept upon one side.

"I did not come here to economise," said Grace, with a grand air, as they took the rooms in Brook Street.

For the first few days Grace was content, and more than content. She did not care about being seen till she was what she called properly dressed, and she certainly knew what she wanted, and got it, as people usually do when they have the command of money.

Then came the grand question of society, and poor Lady Lyons was completely at a standstill.

"Surely you know a few people, Lady Lyons; some one to make a beginning?"

Lady Lyons reflected.

"I have been out of it so long," she murmured; "yes, there is a very kind friend; I wonder if she is in London?"

"Let us find out," said Grace, ringing for the book, and turning over the leaves rapidly. "What is her name?"

"I—I think it begins with a P," said Lady Lyons; "but, dear me, it is so stupid of me. I cannot remember her name at this moment."

"Your kind friend and you have evidently not been corresponding lately," said Grace, laughing.

"My dear Miss Rivers!"

"Now I have got the P's," said Grace, "and I will run through the list."

"Penshurst!" exclaimed Lady Lyons. "Yes, Penshurst is the name."

"There are seventeen," said Grace, in an aggravated tone, "and they live all over London. What *is* Mr. Penshurst?"

"I do not know."

"Ha!" said Grace suddenly, "this is funny. Here is a name Penryn. I used to know one of the girls a little, the daughter of Sir Jacob Penryn, and here is his address. I wonder if she would remember me?"

"Was she at school with you?" asked Lady Lyons, with evident relief.

"Oh! dear no. Her father had a place in the neighbourhood and we went there sometimes, my sister and I, because our father had shown some kindness to a son of his who had died."

"But, my dear, that is a very good thing indeed; write at once, and say you have come into a fortune and are here. A beginning! Why he is an M.P., and has his own house in London."

"No, I will not write," said Grace, decidedly, "and my fortune is hardly worth speaking about, but I will call, and if they wish to renew acquaintance they can return it."

With this Lady Lyons had to be satisfied—indeed, she was more than satisfied, as the difficulty seemed to her to be completely overcome. She took heart now and went off on her own account to see a doctor, and paid a good deal to be assured there was nothing whatever seriously the matter with her.

This was hardly what she had expected or what she anticipated—she was not at all sure she was pleased.

Grace in the meantime left her card, and wrote on the top "In London for a short time with Lady Lyons."

In a few days Miss Penryn called, a very nice-looking girl, dressed with extreme simplicity. She apologized for her mother and brought her card, and an invitation from Lady Penryn for a meeting to be held in her house that week.

When she had left, Grace surveyed her elaborate white toilette and thought her lace frills too numerous.

"It is overdone," she said, discontentedly, to Lady Lyons.

"It is very sweet," said Lady Lyons, who was not thinking of her "young friend's" dress, but who was weighing in her own mind the pros and cons in connection with Lady Penryn's meeting.

She wished to make acquaintance; on the other hand she was terribly afraid of having an appeal made to her pocket, and she was one of many who make small payments to stated charities, and do not like spontaneous action.

Grace settled the point for her, saying with her usual nonchalance,

"You will make your first appearance as my chaperone, Lady Lyons."

After that she could make no objection, but she made many inquiries about Lady Penryn.

"What is she like, my dear? Is she nice?"

"I should say that word describes her exactly; my remembrance of her is that she is much too nice; to be sincere, she always said, 'Dear thing!' and got rid of us as soon as possible."

"She may not have liked children," observed Lady Lyons, lucidly.

"Possibly," but Grace did not think that she was much fonder of grown-up people. She and Margaret had always unfavourably contrasted Lady Penryn's neglect and Sir Jacob's heartiness.

"Gratitude about her son," began Lady Lyons, "that must have been there at any rate."

"Oh! the poor man father knew so well was not her son. She has no son. There were two or three by a first wife; this girl is not her daughter."

When Grace and Lady Lyons arrived in Cromwell Road they found the whole place crowded with people, mostly elderly; a few girls, and the men might be counted on their fingers. Papers were handed to them, and Grace with much amusement found that the meeting was convened about woman's suffrage.

Lady Penryn in a rich crimson velvet was very cordial in her reception of both Lady Lyons and Grace, advised them to sit on the right, said they would find plenty of friends, and turned her back upon them to receive somebody else.

Miss Penryn was not there, or, if there, Grace could not see her.

For upwards of two hours they sat in a room which in spite of open windows was stifling, seated on very small cane chairs, and hearing speeches from men and women more or less celebrated, upon a subject they neither of them took the faintest interest in.

No question of the day ever interested Grace. Lady Lyons never understood the question, and the injustice of women who have large control of money, and who contribute largely to the revenue in many ways and yet cannot give a vote, did not give her a pang. She knew that some women had made the subject ridiculous; she was afraid of ridicule, and she did not take the trouble of disentangling the question from the absurdities reared round it, and judging it on its own merits.

"I don't like being here at all," whispered Lady Lyons; "I am so afraid of being taken for a strong-minded woman."

"Pray do not be afraid of that," said Grace, satirically; "that is the very last thing your worst enemy would accuse you of."

The meeting dragged on, and the heat became quite suffocating. All at once Grace gave a little cry, and threw herself back, closing her eyes.

"A lady fainting! Air! Water! Salts! Salvolatile!" shouted dozens of voices at once.

Grace, still with closed eyes, was carried out of the room, where Lady Lyons gladly remained with her, in a small back room, consecrated to Lady Penryn's writings.

When the meeting dispersed she came in to see how Grace was, and was overwhelming in her affectionate attentions.

"Poor dear thing," she said.

"The heat was very great," said Lady Lyons, apologetically.

"Not in my rooms," said Lady Penryn, very decidedly. "The ventilation is admirably done—a private arrangement of my own."

Lady Lyons was too much awed to contradict her.

"Poor dear thing! how do you feel now?" said Lady Lyons, turning again to Grace.

"I feel better, Lady Lyons, and we will go home," said Grace. "And Lady Penryn, I must apologise for disturbing you all. What funny things everybody said. Do *you* really believe in all that was said to-day?"

Lady Penryn coughed gently.

"My dear, the object of a meeting is to ventilate the subject."

"Oh! I see. Well then, you do not mind my saying that it all struck me as very absurd!"

"The question in itself is not absurd; and it should interest the moneyed class; and it is of general interest."

"Then it should interest me, as I am one of the moneyed class," laughed Grace; "at least, I have an income all to myself."

She was amused to see Lady Penryn look at her with redoubled interest when she made this statement.

"Let us trust, dear child, that you will use your wealth wisely. Now will you not have some tea or wine?" she continued, waxing hospitable.

Lady Lyons accepted, and they went downstairs before they left. Lady Penryn came up to Grace with a good deal of grace, and kissed her on both cheeks.

"For the sake of old times," she said, plaintively.

"She is a sweet young thing," she continued, "and has fulfilled the promise of her youth;" and Grace noted that she took care not to introduce either of the men standing near.

"We will soon meet again, I *trust*," she said, in a pathetic voice.

"That depends upon you," said Grace, quietly. "When you return our visit I hope we shall be at home."

"Ah! till then, good-bye. Sweet thing—good-bye."

"Sweet thing!—good-bye," mimicked Grace, as they got into the brougham.

"Oh! my dear, hush!—some one might hear you."

"Yes, the coachman. I think we had better pursue your Mrs. Penshurst."

"If I could but remember anything about her husband—but I do not. I lay awake for half-an-hour last night, and I cannot recall his Christian name. It may be Charles, but I think it is John—no, it may be James," and Lady Lyons looked blankly before her.

Grace threw herself back in the brougham with a good deal of petulance. They had been three weeks in London and had not achieved a single acquaintance.

As the carriage turned into Brook Street Grace suddenly caught sight of Sir Albert Gerald. She pulled the check-string, and called him by name.

Much surprised, he turned round and came up to her. She was so near Margaret that it was a pleasure to meet her.

"Come and see me," said Grace: "come to tea. This is Lady Lyons. I want particularly to see you—can you come to-morrow?"

"If you could see me early—but I leave town to-morrow afternoon for a few days."

"I will see you at any time. Eleven in the morning will find me clothed and in my right mind, in the stuffy little sitting-room we call our own."

"Till then, good-bye," he said, stepping back, and raising his hat.

"That poor girl looks frightfully ill," he thought, "as if she had not very long to live;" and he went on from this idea to think of Margaret. What a curious difference there was between the two sisters—the one so calm and sweet and so thoughtful, the other so restless and so frivolous.

He kept his word, however, and found Grace in a flutter of spirits, a huge Peerage and the Morning Post in front of her.

It was evident that there was some request trembling on her tongue, and that she was longing for the first conventional phrases to be over; the inquiries about Margaret were answered so indifferently, and Grace was all the time keeping a place in the Peerage open with a finger of her left hand.

"Now, Sir Albert, I do want you to do something for me," she said, with more earnestness than she had yet shown.

"If I can," he said, seriously.

"Yes, you can if you will."

"*Après?*" he asked.

"The Duchess of Mallington is going to give a big 'at-home.' She is your aunt. She is also going to give a ball. Could you not get a card for Lady Lyons and for me to one or other?"

"I think I could," he said; "she's a very dear old lady and I could ask her. She may refuse but I do not think she will."

"Sir Albert, excuse the strength of my language, but you are a darling, there!" exclaimed Grace, laughing and colouring a little. "You do not know how I long to go to just one swell ball, to see it all. It is so dreary moving about in this big place and knowing not one single soul."

"I am sure it must be," said Sir Albert, sympathetically; "it is very natural you should wish to see it all for yourself. I am afraid you will not enjoy it, but I think I can get you the invitation."

"I am sure to enjoy it," and Grace clapped her hands with delight. "Do you not enjoy it?"

"Not much now," he said; "I am very fond of certain people, and I find every one very kind. I like to meet pleasant people in moderation, but I do not go in for much gaiety."

"Only think!" said Grace; "I have never in all my life been to a good, big ball, never!"

"The novelty may amuse you certainly; the only thing is, that if you do not know many people it is very dull looking on and seeing others dancing and talking. If I am there I can take care of you and introduce some men to you at any rate."

"You certainly are a most delightful friend," said Grace, enthusiastically, "and I really do not know how to thank you enough!"

"It is a great pleasure doing anything for you, Miss Rivers. I think you know why!"

"Oh, yes, indeed I do. It is for Margaret."

"Did she tell you I met her accidentally? I got into her railway-carriage without knowing she was there."

"She never told me," said Grace; "Mr. Stevens escorted her till all the changes and junctions and things were passed."

"Who is Mr. Stevens?"

"He was Mr. Drayton's manager, and mixed up in his affairs. I thought you might have seen him at Wandsworth. He came to the rescue at that terrible time."

"I saw no one but *her* then," he said, in a lower voice. "Miss Rivers, do you think she will forget all that frightful business?"

"I think she will: at least, her letters are much less heart-broken than they were. I think she rather nursed her sorrow at Wandsworth. Then she took to going to see sick children and giving away all her money, and she began to get better."

"She gave away all her money?"

"Every farthing he left her. Yes, she would not keep even one hundred pounds a year, nor a hundred pence. She could not bear touching his money."

"I am so glad!" he said, fervently.

"Really?" Grace said, in a curious tone.

Sir Albert coloured, and said,

"It is pleasant when a character we admire is consistent."

"Margaret is very consistent."

"She is everything a high-minded woman should be," he answered, earnestly; "I am quite sure we agree in our ideas of her."

"Perhaps we do; but you express it better than I do: and my sister is too good for *me.* I admire her, but she is so far above me that there is not full sympathy between us."

"But there might be," he said, in his quiet voice; "to live with some one having a high aim must help one."

"It does not help me," said Grace, sharply, but with an accent of pain in her voice; throwing off any feeling weighing with her she added, in a laughing tone, "It gives me a crick in my neck."

She puzzled him. It was painful to him to see her so delicate and thinking of nothing but amusement, but he could not judge; and through the flippant tone broke so much real feeling that he knew she spoke much more lightly than she felt. She was Margaret's sister, and he would do his utmost for her amusement. Instead of leaving London as he had intended doing, he would remain and go to this ball and to others, and do his utmost to enable her to enjoy it.

The Duchess's card and the invitation were handed to Lady Lyons; and her first idea was that it was a mistake. Grace interposed.

"It is all right, Lady Lyons; of course the Duchess could not ask me without you, and I know some of her family."

Lady Lyons was most deeply impressed.

"My dear! I never was in the same room with a duchess before; it is very delightful."

"l do not suppose she is different from other people," said Grace, indifferently.

"I hope it is not a case of a new gown—I really cannot afford it," and Lady Lyons looked really troubled.

"As I am dragging you to the party, I will find the gown," said Grace, laughing; "leave it to me."

This card was not the only one that came on that and the following days, and Grace was quite enchanted, though she professed to be prepared for this, and any thing else that might befall her.

Lady Lyons was not quite happy. She was by nature indolent, and she was easily fatigued. Women who assume the habits of an invalid, soon become invalids in reality. She loved going to bed at nine o'clock and being read to sleep; indeed, with a vague idea that Grace intended to make herself useful to her, she had said something about the reading, and the peculiarities of her maid's pronunciation, but Grace was too wise to begin by doing anything that might be a tax upon her in future, and she laughed the idea to scorn—"besides," she added, and with truth, "with my delicate chest, the exertion would be very bad for me."

But, as Lady Lyons loved going to bed early, the prospect of being out of it for an indefinite number of hours was not amusing; still the thoughts of seeing so many people, known only through the newspapers, sustained her.

She gave many sighs, however, in private; Grace half thought of persuading her to go to bed early in the afternoon, but for a well-founded conviction that, if she did, she would in all probability not get up again; but she did get her to drink strong coffee, and that, and the sight of her new dress, kept her comfortably awake.

Grace appeared, radiant, her inexperience making her punctual. She had a very simple white gown, and looked well.

When they arrived they found themselves very nearly the first, and quite the first of the strangers asked.

Lady Lyons looked about for the great lady and could not see her. At that moment a kind little old lady held out her hand—asked the black and white gentleman doubling himself in two before her to repeat the names, and Lady Lyons and Miss Withers was the result shouted into her Grace's deaf ears.

Grace was half annoyed and half amused. She went to a sofa near, and sat down watching the arrivals, and being entertained by the talk going on between a plain clever looking girl, with a quantity of red hair, and some older girls, who stood caressing their elbows in the doorway very affectionately.

"The dear Duchess has a funnier mixture than ever, to-night, apparently," said the eldest maiden, who had on a crushed looking dress, and who used an eyeglass very freely when she neglected her elbows for a moment.

"Yes, dear old thing! she is so kind-hearted, she never can say no. You cannot conceive anything so funny as the mob coming to-night."

"What makes her do it?"

"Good-nature; she says people like to come because she has a big house, and can give them a good supper, and why should she not?" and the girl laughed.

"She is rather a trial in some things. You have no idea how young men fly her. She is so sorry for plain girls that she marches them up, whether they like it or not, and introduces them straight off. I assure you she has carried off my pet partners under my very eyes, and made them dance with lamp-posts and billiard-balls."

"My dear," whispered Lady Lyons in a very discreet whisper, "what does she mean by that? How can a man dance with——?"

"Oh! do you really not understand?" said Grace, impatiently; "tall girls and very short ones."

"Oh!" and Lady Lyons drew a very long breath.

No band, no music, and hardly any men. It was going to be a very queer ball, Grace thought. An hour and a half passed in this way. As a rule, people wore gowns that had seen the brunt of the season—no one was very smart except as regarded jewels. A great many people had beautiful diamonds on, and some had good lace, but the majority, knowing what a crowd there would be, had left lace at home.

The band arrived and began playing two or three bars of well-known valses and then stopping. Then, all at once, there was a sudden stream of people, the rooms filled all at once, and dancing began. But only in a limited space; it began all over the large room, three or four circles beginning at once.

The sound of the music, the sight of others doing what she would like to do, filled Grace with despair. She did not know a soul, and nobody looked at her or noticed her in any way. Dance after dance went on, and the girl felt really forlorn—tears of vexation rose in her eyes and nearly overflowed.

Lady Lyons fidgeted.

"I think the Duchess might find you a partner," she said, huffily; "and what an uncomfortable sofa! I wish for my part that I was safe at home again."

And Grace very nearly said,

"So do I!"

A funny looking little man, with curiously small eyes and a big head, passed and re-passed, looking along the benches, sliding behind the crowd, which seemed to increase every moment. As he passed he saw Grace's wistful eyes, and he went on.

Returning, he was accompanied by a tall fine looking, middle-aged man; they approached, and her heart beat high with hope; this little man was some relation, and he had found her a partner.

Delightful delusion born to be dispelled. The tall man bowed to Lady Lyons, and then said,

"Her Grace has asked me to introduce Mr. Bott to you and your niece; he is anxious to persuade her to try this valse;" and without seeing Grace (unless, as she thought angrily, he could see her without looking at her) he bowed himself away again.

Grace's mortification knew no bounds. To make her first public appearance dancing with this peculiar looking man was very terrible to her, but to sit for a whole evening behind the backs (and very ample backs) of sundry dowagers, who either preferred standing or could find no seats to their liking, seemed the only other alternative, and still more intolerable to her.

She rose and moved with him, a little surprised at the way he glided through the dense crowd, making room for her behind him.

She had been considered at school a perfect dancer, but dancing well with mankind requires practice which she had never had, and this little man danced abominably. He had all possible defects, and did as nearly as he could every single thing he ought not to have done.

He could not steer. He had no confidence, and he got out of nobody's way. Grace's ears got red and tingled, and her whole face flushed with wounded vanity.

After two or three struggles, in which they were ignominiously worsted, she stopped and gazed at the soft, gliding motion of happier girls, with a feeling of anger and desperation.

Then coming towards her, she saw a couple moving with an inexpressibly graceful air, and recognised Sir Albert Gerald.

Forgetful of everything, but that she saw at last one face she knew, she stepped forward and pronounced his name.

Sir Albert laughingly bowed and swung on without stopping.

Tears rose in her eyes, and, turning to Mr. Bott, she said—

"I do not feel well. Will you take me to Lady Lyons?"

He obeyed in silence, so deeply offended with her for her manner, showed evident want of appreciation or his dancing, that he made no effort to persuade her to have some refreshment instead, and bowing, turned away immediately.

"Let us go home, Lady Lyons; I am so tired."

"And have no supper! I have been longing to have something to eat. I declare, sitting on this hard bench and doing penance, makes one desperately hungry; and I am here on your account, my dear."

"How can we go to supper without any one to take us?"

"We can go by ourselves—several people have done it already—do come."

Just as Grace was complying with her request, she was stopped by Sir Albert Gerald, who brought a young man—a very young man—up to Grace, and introduced him.

"I am coming to claim a dance soon," he said; "I saw you suffering martyrdom with poor little Bott. It was very good of you to give him a dance."

"I could not help myself," said Grace, her spirits restored immediately by this change in her prospects of enjoyment; "he was the only person introduced to me."

"Bott always manages to find a new victim," said the man introduced by Sir Albert—a Mr. Powis. "Do you want to have supper? Oh! I see, the old lady does. Come along, Gerald; we will have supper all together," and Lady Lyons was soon as perfectly happy as she could be while half dead from want of sleep.

CHAPTER VII.

The appearance of Sir Albert Gerald on the scene of action had a magical effect upon Grace. Every trace of fatigue vanished. She was once again bright, happy, careless, and full of enjoyment; once again the music charmed her, and once again she was glad to be there.

Supper over, Sir Albert found a more comfortable seat for Lady Lyons, and introduced her to a lady sitting there, who eyed her smart clothes with a little suspicion till the Duchess addressed a few kind words to her, when she discovered immediately that they had much in common.

Lady Lyons indeed was overflowing with content to find some one to talk to, after prolonged silence, in the first place; and, in the next, to discover that they had been disappointed in the same doctor, liked the same food, and had the same symptoms; this made the ball enjoyable indeed, and she did not care now how long Grace stayed.

In the meantime Grace realised her dreams; she floated round the room, though her appearance was a little marred by the peculiar position of her head and a certain stiffness in her action.

"You must trust more to me and be a little less timid," said Mr. Powis, when he, in his turn, took her round the room; "one can see you are out of practice."

Grace did not tell *him* it was quite her first ball.

She danced without stopping; she would not take it quietly; she did want this one ball to be full of happiness, and she was encouraged by the laughing compliments of young Powis, who, himself a noted athlete and in excellent condition, could have danced for hours, and, to use his own expression, "not turn a hair."

Grace's lips got very white, and Sir Albert more than once remonstrated with her and with her partner.

"Has Gerald got anything to do with you?" he asked, with some temper. "What makes him interfere?"

"I am sure I don't know," Grace answered with a ghastly smile; "but you see I don't mind. Let us go on."

"What a brick you are!" he said, as they once more started. Arrived at the end of the long room, there was suddenly a great commotion, and Mr. Powis was shocked to find his "brick" of a partner fall back in a perfectly dead faint, in the arms of some of those lookers-on always standing about in a ball-room.

She was quickly carried into a small sitting-room, where they scattered one or two people holding interesting conversations there.

There was one chief idea present to every one, the Duchess must not be disturbed and the ball not for a second interrupted.

Grace was very long coming round, and then she owned herself too ill to stay.

Lady Lyons was found without much difficulty, and the two left the brilliant scene as soon as possible.

Young Powis said something about the catastrophe to Sir Albert, who was annoyed with him.

"How could I know she was going to faint?" he said; "she seemed all right: she wanted to go on."

"She has been very ill indeed for months, and, as I sent her the invitation, I felt bound to try and prevent her from doing herself harm."

"Oh, I did not know. She goes well enough, but she hangs back and makes herself heavy; my arm aches enough now. All the same I am very sorry. I could not think why you interfered."

"If it had not been you it would have been with somebody else," and Sir Albert sprang into a hansom and disappeared.

Lady Lyons only knew that Grace was over-fatigued; she knew nothing of her having fainted, and Grace herself was quite determined to say as little as possible. Were there not several other cards waiting, offering the same enjoyment?

In the manner a stupid woman sometimes has of vexing unintentionally, poor Lady Lyons contrived to offend her a good deal.

"Really, my dear, you cannot be grateful enough to that nice Sir Albert Gerald. But for him you and I would have had no supper, no dancing, and a very dull evening; and he hunted up a partner for you as well as dancing with you himself. I assure you he took a lot of trouble about it."

"Mr. Powis asked to be introduced to me."

"Did he, my dear? Why, what a humbug he must be! I heard him myself say to Sir Albert, '*I know too many girls already; do let me off!*' and Sir Albert said, 'Nonsense,' and walked him up to you, and then he pretended to wish it himself."

"At any rate Sir Albert said, 'Mr. Powis would like to be introduced to you,'" and Grace was red with anger and mortification.

"My dear, I think they always say that. I heard it said so often near me."

Grace was silent. She had thought that this one man had been attracted by her, forgetting that in a great crowd there must be that undeniable *something* to be at all noticed.

Her next ball was a great mortification to her. She saw Mr. Powis, he asked her how she was, hoped she was better, and did *not* ask her to dance; more than this, he expressed surprise at her coming to a ball again.

"I should have thought you would have funked it, Miss Rivers. I shall feel quite nervous till I see you going home, you know."

Grace was furious.

She and poor Lady Lyons sat on unnoticed. They went away when they were tired and crept into the supper-room.

All the servants of the establishment were drawn up in a phalanx in the hall in splendid liveries, and the supper—done by contract—was very bad, and the waiters worse. They sat very forlorn, getting no attention, and retreated, nearly worn out, and having the greatest difficulty in getting their carriage, none of the liveries choosing to face a drizzling rain and call it up. After standing very long in a terrible draught, some one asked the name, and "Lady Lyons's carriage, no servant!" was shouted up and down the street.

Grace burst out laughing, but Lady Lyons, who saw nothing funny in any part of the evening's entertainment, subsided in a heap in the corner of the brougham and wept.

In spite of this, Grace persisted in going to the few things offered her.

"I cannot understand your caring for going out; you never meet a soul you know. Why do you go?" cried poor Lady Lyons at last.

"I go because it is so good for me—and for you too."

"So good for you! So good for me!"

"Yes, it is a sort of penance for you, sitting there and not amusing yourself; and, as for me," said Grace, lightly, "after this I can never set too high a value on myself! It is mortification all round."

"You say the oddest things."

"I am glad I am original; and now, Lady Lyons, I want to arrange some business, and when that is done I want to go to Scotland, but I must finish my business first."

"How long will it take?" asked Lady Lyons.

"I cannot tell. I want to make my will."

"My dear!"

"Is that another original idea? People have done such a thing before. Why do you particularly want to know about the time, Lady Lyons? You very clever people always have a motive in asking anything."

"It is about the rooms, my dear, and it is about my son," and Lady Lyons looked at Grace to see whether this mention of her son's name had any interest for her.

Grace hardly heard her. She was conscious herself of being very much worse in health than she had been when she arrived in London. It was true she had met many mortifications, but she did not care much about them. She had seen something of that whirl she had longed to be in, though she was conscious she had only been at the edge and looking on from a distance. The disenchantment, however, was complete; she saw that, unless living and moving amongst people and having them as friends, there was no pleasure in going to any place, however brilliant; and she was struck with the higher tone of many of the people she met, who did not live only for pleasure, but who took interest in other things, and who accepted "excitement" as an interruption, even if a pleasant interruption, to their usual pursuits, and did not make it their business. She grew ashamed of the frivolous aims and small ambitions she had, and, though she did not own it to herself, she wished she was more like Margaret.

Sir Albert called one day to say good-bye. He was going abroad. He wanted very much to say something to Grace, but he wanted to speak to her alone, and Lady Lyons was always there.

That good woman's way of thanking him for the trouble he had taken to promote their amusement was very amusing.

"Yes, indeed, Sir Albert, but for you, as I always say to Miss Rivers, no supper, no partners, a hard bench and a crowd. Oh, dear! I shall never forget it, never! Then you came, and that supper, and the Duchess was civil, and I had a pleasant conversation, and all was different."

"I am very glad I was able to be of use. The Duchess is always kind."

"Yes, she is very kind—though I bowed to her yesterday and she did not know me; perhaps, as I had a very thick veil on she could not see me," Lady Lyons added reflectively.

"Perhaps not."

"There is only one thing, Sir Albert, if you don't mind my saying it—I was so surprised to see her so plain."

"So plain! We think, in the family, that my aunt, for her age, is very good-looking; she has such a pleasant face."

"Oh! I don't mean plain in the sense of ugly," Lady Lyons said, in a great hurry, "but plain in her dress. She had no jewels on, not even a diamond ring, for I looked to see when she took off her gloves at supper."

"Some people think that the hostess ought to be unadorned. I rather like the sentiment."

"I don't the least understand it," said Lady Lyons, bluntly; "when I used to have company I put on my smartest gown."

"I suppose the Duchess has no smartest gowns," he answered laughing.

"Now that's nonsense, Sir Albert. But I should like to know the 'sentiment,' as you call it, though, for my own part, I cannot see any connection between sentiment and clothes."

"I do," said Grace; "if I am in a very good temper I can wear blue or white with a quiet conscience; if I am in a rage I wear red."

"My dear Miss Rivers! You do say such funny things."

"I shall then avoid speaking to you if I see you in a red gown," laughed Sir Albert.

"You had better——but please enlighten Lady Lyons, she is dying to know why one's 'best' gowns should not be aired on grand occasions."

"I fancy the idea is that it is better taste not to outshine one's guests," Sir Albert said; "the Duchess has such magnificent jewels that it would be easy to outdo every one else."

"That is rather a delicate nice feeling," said Grace, warmly.

"But I would rather wear my jewels, if I had any," said Lady Lyons. "Sir Albert, did you notice my butterfly the other night? No! how strange! Well, never mind! I will go and get it for you, it has a history."

She left the room, and Sir Albert seized his opportunity. "Miss Rivers," he began, hurriedly, "you have some idea, have you not, of what your sister is to me?"

"I think I have" said Grace demurely.

"Will you do me a very great kindness?" he said, earnestly. "Will you send me a line now and again? All that dreadful time the only plan, for *her* sake, was to keep away."

"I suppose it was," said Grace; "it must have been difficult."

"It has been very difficult."

"And when I send you this line, 'now and again,' am I to say anything to her?"

"I see no reason you should not let her know you are so kind as to write to me," he answered.

"Nor do I. I only wanted to know."

"If at any time you think she would care to see me—if I could ever be of use—you will let me know?"

"I will. Not that sending a letter to Norway or Finland, let alone the Antipodes, holds out much prospect of your being able to come within a reasonable time," she added, laughing.

"Distance sounds more than it is," he answered, composedly, "and I may not go quite so far as the Antipodes."

"Or Norway?" she said, mischievously.

He coloured vividly.

"Miss Rivers, I mean to put the sea between us, till...."

"Till she has forgotten, in some measure," said Grace, kindly. "I think you are right; because, just now, everything is so terrible to her. She might think happiness in connection with you quite out of the question; and if you came forward just now she might put herself into a position from which it might be difficult for her to draw back. I think you must wait till she has quite recovered, and then she may become conscious of a great blank in her life, and wish for you."

"God grant it may be so!" he said, fervently.

"Do you mind telling me how it was it all went wrong at Lornbay? I thought you cared for her then."

"Cared for her! It was a terrible misunderstanding. I never can forgive myself for having said something—put something in a stupid way. It does not bear thinking about. You have no conception what a trial *that* has been to bear. It has added to everything else."

"Well, before my lady and her butterfly comes, hear me promise to do what little I can in the matter, Sir Albert. Let us swear an eternal friendship!"

She held out her hand as Lady Lyons came into the room, and he gave her a grateful pressure. Lady Lyons coughed loudly, as much as to say—"I am here."

"Now, Sir Albert," said Grace, gaily, "Lady Lyons is quite shocked; you really must not make love to me under her very eyes."

Poor Lady Lyons felt dreadfully taken aback. Sir Albert, however, was so kind about her jewel, and, taking it to the light, gave it such real attention, that she was soon thinking of her butterfly more than of anything else.

When he had gone, however, the little scene recurred to her, and she began talking about him.

She was just sufficiently afraid of Grace to begin the conversation as far from the subject as possible, and, without losing sight of what she wanted to know, she began talking of Mrs. Dorriman, and of the days of her youth, when she had been a neglected girl of sixteen as Anne Sandford.

"Do you know, my dear, that in those days people used to think she was an heiress. Nobody knew anything at all about the brother, and it was such a surprise when he appeared. No one knew anything about *his* mother, and no one, I believe—none of his most intimate friends—knew of his father's first marriage."

"A disagreeable surprise for Mrs. Dorriman."

"Yes! and how good she is always; never a murmur, and it is very hard for her. First of all, her father made no will; then her husband muddled away all his money! Poor dear woman! Now, can any one say truthfully that she has had a happy life?" And Lady Lyons looked round the room, appealing, as it were, to an invisible audience, only at last looking at Grace.

"It is quite impossible that any one should be happy without independence," answered Grace. "It is a most galling thing to owe all, or nearly all, to some one who is nothing to one. I speak feelingly, Lady Lyons. Mr. Sandford, out of affection for his wife (who, as you know, was my aunt), offered us a home, and added to our income at school. But he made the obligation hateful to us by the way he went on. His temper is absolutely unbearable. I cannot tell you how terrible the scenes were. No one—no girl with any sense of self-respect—could put up with it! No one!"

"My dear! this is very, very sad."

"It is more than sad. This is the history of my poor darling Margaret's marriage. I was so utterly wretched, so perfectly miserable, that she married Mr. Drayton (all her instincts being against him) to save *me* from a life I hated. I urged her to do it; but, Lady Lyons, I was very ill; if I had only been well—if only I had not felt so much in want of all the comfort and care I could get—I am sure I never would have allowed her to sacrifice herself so terribly."

She stopped, exhausted, and covered her face with her hands.

"My dear! my dear!" said Lady Lyons, feebly patting her on the arm. "For my sake do not excite yourself so much. I am so very sorry I brought this forward—but I don't think I did either."

"It does not matter whether you did or not, it is always here—no, not always," said Grace, with a bitter little laugh, "because I am not a girl who makes herself miserable about what cannot be helped, but when I am driven into thought——Oh! Lady Lyons, do you know what it is? Did you ever, in all your life, have remorse?"

"Oh, yes!" said Lady Lyons, very placidly, "when I lost my husband I wished I had not been so cross to him. But he was trying, my dear—very trying. However, I was sorry I was snappish to him sometimes. It quite weighed upon me when he died."

Grace laughed again, and Lady Lyons looked at her curiously. What had she said that was so funny? She began to talk again, this time a little spitefully.

"I suppose you will be glad if your sister marries again?"

"Of course, I shall be glad for her to do whatever is for her happiness; but marrying again, Lady Lyons, does it not seem a little hard that she should have so many chances and I ... have none?"

"My dear, if I am not very much mistaken, Sir Albert Gerald is very much in love."

"Yes, I think he is very much in love," Grace answered indifferently.

"Then let us hope it will all come right."

"I hope it will," and before Lady Lyons could go on with her investigations a servant came to ask if Grace would see Mr. Stevens.

"Certainly." Grace was enchanted to see any one; and Lady Lyons, who did not care for Mr. Stevens, carefully gathered her patchwork together and left the room.

"Well, Mr. Stevens, you see me on the very verge of departure," exclaimed Grace; "I am really going far from this gay and festive scene, and intend recruiting my shattered nerves in Highland air."

Mr. Stevens looked at her gravely. He was deeply shocked by her appearance. She looked so fragile, and her lips were so absolutely without colour.

"I hope the Highland air will set you up," he said; "you look as if you have not had sleep for an indefinite time."

"No, sleep.... I do not sleep well." There was something almost pathetic in her tone. He had seen her pretty often now, but he had always seen her full of high spirits, bandying words; he thought her more interesting, and he said very kindly, "Change of air does much for every one, and it will do you good seeing your sister."

"How is she?" Grace felt softened by his tone.

"A different person since she went there. I went up there for a few days...." A curious hesitation in his manner struck her.

"I shall like being with my sister. I shall very much dislike being with some one else," Grace said, with a bitterness of tone he could not help noticing.

"Not—Mrs. Dorriman?"

"Not—Mrs. Dorriman!" she rejoined, imitating the little pause he had made, and looking at him with laughing eyes.

Mr. Stevens got up and looked out of the window. Grace called him back. "Did you come to see how I was? I do not look very robust, but I intend to get well up in the North."

"I hope you will."

"But you are afraid? Mr. Stevens, your face is nearly as good as a looking-glass. I see exactly how I look by the expression of your eyebrows. When you come into the room they are tidy and straight; if I look well they arch up into a sort of surprised state, as much as to say 'That girl is a riddle to me, she is actually better, who would have thought it?' When I look very ill, as I suppose I look to-day, they go down in a melancholy line and say as plainly as possible, 'Poor thing! she is going down-hill very fast.'"

"Miss Rivers, I am sorry my eyebrows should be so very inconveniently expressive," he said, trying to laugh, and feeling absolutely heartsick; she seemed to him frightfully ill, and so utterly devoid of anything like serious thought.

"You need not be sorry," she said, in an odd tone; "we none of us know anything of each other, and I daresay I judge you quite as hardly as you do me."

"Hardly! Do I judge you hardly?"

"You think I am so fearfully frivolous and thoughtless and——I cannot at this moment think of any other words."

"I know your sister best. She is not thoughtless: and may I say to you, Miss Rivers, that the more I know her the more thunderstruck I am at her ever having married poor Drayton?"

"You knew him better than any of us."

"Yes, ever since his boyhood. He had no chance. His father and mother were cousins, and insanity in the family. It was terrible to me to hear of his marriage."

Grace shivered.

"You do not like Mr. Sandford. I remember hearing this. I cannot bear him."

"He is in very bad health now."

"That does not alter things a bit. When I think of all his rudeness and violence ... and he always looks to me as though he had some great sin lying on his conscience."

Grace watched Mr. Stevens very narrowly, and she saw him give a little start.

He turned the subject at once.

"I came to pay something over to you, Miss Rivers—will you give me a receipt?"

It was a large cheque—the interest on the fifteen thousand pounds from the date of her sister's marriage.

"Mrs. Drayton refused this—the legacy duty is deducted and an account inclosed."

Grace examined it all quietly. Then she drew a blotting-book near her. She signed a receipt and inclosed the cheque to her bankers—rang, and desired the letter to be sent by hand.

Mr. Stevens watched her narrowly; how curiously unlike Mrs. Drayton she was, and yet something—that indescribable and subtle resemblance which comes out in tricks of manner more than in feature—would have caused Grace to be known any where as Margaret's sister. He began to describe Inchbrae to her, but she stopped him hurriedly.

"Pray do not begin about it for I know it by heart—Margaret writes about nothing else, and, as for Mrs. Dorriman, I do not know whether she or Jean talk most about it. Clear crystal sea—soft shadows on the mountains, sometimes clouds (always clouds *I* should say!)—sharp crags, fir-trees beautiful with red stems, beautiful without, waterfall, rowan-trees, scarlet geraniums, *and* a grey house. There, do I know my lesson, or do I not? The idea of your beginning too!"

Mr. Stevens went off into a fit of laughter, and he was one of the men who laughed with merriment, so many are noisy and not merry. In the midst of this hilarity in walked a tall young man announcing himself, with an injured waiter in the background waving deprecating hands.

It was Paul Lyons.

"Come and laugh too, Mr. Lyons," said Grace, as she shook hands with him. "Should you be surprised to hear that Mr. Stevens (by the way, let me introduce you. Mr. Stevens, Mr. Lyons; the same to the same). Yes, Mr. Stevens is laughing at an excellent, undeniable joke made by me."

Paul Lyons seemed older and more careworn than when she had last seen him. He looked at her with so grave an expression that she was startled. The laughter died away upon her lips, and she was silent.

"You have been ill?"

He spoke with very real feeling, and she, though she tried to answer him lightly, the effort was a failure. At length she said shortly—

"I have been ill, and your mother kind. My face speaks for itself, I suppose."

"Yes," answered Paul, "you are looking far from well. But you are better? You are going away?"

"Who told you this important fact?"

"My mother. I came home sooner. I wanted to see you before you went away."

Mr. Stevens had not very quick perceptions, but when Paul Lyons made this speech it dawned upon him that he was perhaps in the way.

He rose, and, renewing his offers of service, left the room, with an overpowering amount of thanks from Grace.

"Tell me about your illness, now that man has gone. Have you been seriously ill—as ill as my mother thinks?"

"How can I possibly tell what your mother thinks?"

"Oh, Grace! do not trifle just now! I have known for a very long time that my whole happiness is bound up in you!"

"Margaret is free, remember."

"What does that matter? Why remind me that I once liked her best? Is a man never to change? I know now—I have long known it—if I could but get you to believe it! that Margaret was a sort of dream of my youth. I shall always reverence her, but she is too far beyond me. She is like some pure cold saint, and I do love you, Grace!"

"But I have no wealth to endow you with," said Grace, looking at him earnestly, "only a very few hundreds a year."

She watched him a little anxiously, but his face showed it did not matter.

"I am poor enough," he said, "but you shall never want anything if you will only give me the right of taking care of you. I have succeeded in getting an appointment in Italy. I am sure that climate will suit you; the doctors said so."

"And you got the appointment without knowing that I would say yes," exclaimed Grace, a good deal in her old manner.

"If you say no, all places will be alike to me."

"Oh, Paul! shall I tell you something? I do love you, but I have a great deal to say to you before I say yes or no."

"Say anything now, and put me out of suspense."

"I believe I shall live; I am not very strong; but I am stronger than people think; and Paul, if I do say yes—if I am your wife—I am afraid you will have a very sorry bargain. I am not a very amiable girl, and I am capricious. Do you know what I am afraid of? I am always so afraid of getting tired of my husband."

"Grace, please don't talk like this. I also have many faults; you do not think I am perfect, do you? We must make allowances for each other."

"I certainly do not think you perfect," said Grace, laughing a little, "but I do think you should reflect. Just think, Paul: a delicate wife, full of whims, not very attractive."

"Grace, you will drive me crazy if you go on in this way. I love you, dear, with all your whims, and all else, and you will get strong and well in Italy. Say plainly, and at once, that you will marry me."

"Well then, plainly and at once, I will, Paul. I am not quite sure that the reason I care for you is not that you are the only man who has ever wished to marry me, but I will only marry you on one condition."

"On any condition, darling."

"I want to be married at once. I have heaps of new clothes; and I do not want to go to Scotland and confront old Sandford without some one to fight my battles."

Paul was surprised to find his mother pleased about his marriage.

"I was afraid you wanted me to marry a rich wife," he said, his satisfaction unbounded at the evident pleasure with which she received his news.

"I did, Paul, yes; but Grace has something."

"Not much I am afraid—but I have this appointment, mother, and we shall get on all right."

"I suppose it is not much; did she tell you what it was?"

"A few hundreds."

"A year. She has six or seven hundred a year."

"Oh!" said Paul, "I am glad, mother, of course. I am also glad I did not know anything about it."

"Would it have made a difference?"

"I cannot say," he answered.

CHAPTER VIII.

Lady Lyons was in a great state of excitement about Grace's wedding. She had large ideas as to what was the right thing to do; and she never for one moment thought that upon an occasion of this kind Grace would be wilful or obstinate. That she was peculiar she knew; but she had no idea she would indulge in peculiar ideas about a wedding, and that wedding her own.

Grace would have no wedding-cake, no breakfast (in that sense), and no fuss, no bridesmaids. It was to be by special licence, and quiet as quiet could be.

"But why, my dear?"

"Because there is no one to ask."

"We have plenty of acquaintances. I know many people, and it is unusual to have a wedding in a corner this way."

"I don't know about a corner—I am to be married in church."

"You know what I mean, Grace; and it is my only son."

"I am sorry you have not got more sons, if you wish it, Lady Lyons."

Then suddenly she knelt down beside her and said earnestly—

"Usually there are friends to rejoice; there is a mother or sisters, a father—some one who cares for a girl. They gather round her at an important moment of her life; but, Lady Lyons, in all the world there does not exist a more forlorn girl than I am. It would be mockery to summon acquaintances and call them friends. What do they know about me or about your son? I have thought, till I am tired of thinking, who there is to give me away. I can think of no one—I shall have to borrow a father for the occasion; and I cannot think where I shall find one."

"My dear Grace, you do say such odd things!"

"Do I? I am speaking the truth, perhaps that seems odd."

"I do not feel as if it would be a wedding at all."

"I hope it will be a wedding, though there are to be no guests; and, without guests to eat it, why have a wedding-cake?"

"To send some away, and the look of the thing. You don't seem to think of that."

"Who is to look? There is to be no one. I do not care for wedding-cake myself, though I love the almond-paste, and, if you eat some, you would be ill for weeks."

Lady Lyons was not to be consoled. She told Sir Albert (who was still detained in town), and he tried to sympathise with her. Then he spoke to Grace—

"If people came, not here, but to the church—you would not mind it?"

"How can I prevent people from going to church?"

"And who is to give you away?"

"I do not know; I have told Lady Lyons I intend borrowing a father for the occasion."

"How would Sir Jacob do?"

"They have never been near us, though they made such a fuss about us. Of course, it is not *his* fault—still I will not ask him."

"It would be kinder to think of some one, and so please Lady Lyons."

"But, kind or not kind, I cannot think of any one."

"There is some one I know; he is very kind, and it would be pleasanter for you."

"It would be much better if I knew some one. I think girls are to be envied who have relations and friends; I have none."

"If I find some one will you be nice about it?"

"I will be very nice: as nice as I know to be. Lady Lyons would like some one a little before the world. She thinks Paul's wedding a very important thing."

"If I can I will arrange about it. I was so provoked about not getting away, now I am glad."

"Yes, I am Margaret's sister."

"You say she is not coming?"

"She offered and I declined. Where was the use of a long journey? I am going north afterwards."

"And you are to write to me?"

"If Paul is not jealous," and she laughed.

Then he said good-bye.

That evening Lady Lyons sat worrying herself a good deal about everything in general, and this impending difficulty in particular, when a note to Grace was brought in. It was from the Duchess.

"DEAR MISS RIVERS,

"My nephew says that, owing to your sister's absence, you would like to be befriended a little on your wedding-day. The Duke begs me to say that he will give you away with pleasure, and, as Lady Lyons is the young man's mother, I will call and take you to church.

"How wise you are to have no bridesmaids or breakfast. I wish other girls were as sensible. Believe me, dear Miss Rivers,

"Yours truly,

"KATHERINE MALLINGTON."

Grace gave the note to Lady Lyons without comment.

"Her Grace's servant waits to see if there is any answer," said the waiter, very respectfully.

Grace wrote,

"DEAR DUCHESS OF MALLINGTON,

"You are very kind, and I beg to thank you and the Duke very much. Yes, I shall be very grateful to you for so befriending me; it is good of you, who know me so little; of course it is also good of your nephew.

"Yours truly,

"GRACE RIVERS."

"My dear Grace, now all is most delightfully arranged," said Lady Lyons; "now it will not be in a corner."

"The place is not changed," said Grace. "I told you before I did not mean a corner."

"You do take everything so much as a matter of course," said Lady Lyons, irritably.

"How ought I to take things? Ought I to laugh or cry? Tell me what is the proper thing to do?"

"You might be a little pleased."

"I am very much pleased. I think the Duchess is very kind."

"She must have taken a fancy to you, my dear."

"I think not. I suspect she does not know me by sight."

"Then why do this? What do you think yourself?"

"I think it is all for Margaret."

"And she has never seen her! My dear, you really are too ridiculous!"

"No, Lady Lyons; can you not see how things really are? Sir Albert knew how you lamented my want of friends and he has done this for me."

"But why, my dear, why? That's what I want to know," and Lady Lyons looked puzzled.

"Ah, that is very puzzling indeed," said Grace, gravely: and Lady Lyons, who had from the first stated that she thought she had a gown that was quite good enough, went to consult her maid upon the subject.

She found her maid in a state of ecstacy over a very handsome dark, plum-coloured silk, very fashionably though quietly made, bonnet and mantle to match, "With Grace's love" on the top of it.

"Oh, my dear, how lovely! I am so sorry I said that about a corner. Corner, indeed! how kind, how very thoughtful of you! I cannot bear taking such a handsome present from you."

"You must learn to take many presents from your new daughter," said Grace, but something in her tone struck Lady Lyons.

"You have been crying," she exclaimed; "what is it, my dear? what has happened?"

"Nothing has happened, but I have a letter from Margaret, a most dear letter, and I could not help contrasting my marriage with hers, for I love Paul, Lady Lyons, and all is different."

"Very different," said Lady Lyons, and she sighed sympathetically; "and Mr. Drayton had no position, my dear; he was only a manufacturer."

"Oh, Lady Lyons, how absurd you are!" said Grace, the tears still standing in her eyes, though she laughed heartily; "fancy, in these days, talking like that! Why, all our leading spirits in Parliament and out of it are 'only' manufacturers; they have the ball at their feet now."

"My dear, you have a way of putting things I never can follow," said poor Lady Lyons; "now you are talking about a ball, it is really very puzzling."

"Well then, I beg your pardon over and over and over again," said Grace, "and I will try not to say puzzling things."

"Thank you, my dear," said Lady Lyons, very heartily, who considered this a great concession.

"Now I am to be your daughter," said the girl, with the natural wish of having a little affection and kindness shown to her just now, "you will try and like me—love me a little bit." She looked wistfully at Lady Lyons, who was touched and quite melted by this appeal.

"I suppose," she said very naïvely to Grace, who had turned round to leave the room, "that I also have things about me, peculiarities that require indulgence."

"You are very good," said Grace, evading the question, "and I mean to be a good wife to Paul, you believe that?"

"Oh, yes, my dear, indeed, you put that very prettily; I used to wish it was Margaret, but now I think you will like to know, that I am quite reconciled—then there is the Duchess, and my new dress!"

Grace laughed a little and left her.

She locked her door and once again read Margaret's affectionate, earnest letter.

After discussing the news of her marriage she said,

"Now, Grace, my darling, I want you to think, think more prayerfully than I did, about this. If you do not love Paul Lyons, do not mind the disagreeable speeches that may be made, but do not go on with it. Far better to bear angry words now than to marry without love. I would come to you, darling, at a moment's notice, and I could make a home for you somewhere, only do not do this. Had I had so solemn a warning I might have been saved."

There was more to the same point; each word, every line, showed by its intensity what an agony of pain, and shame, and misery she had herself gone through.

Hot tears fell on Grace's hands as she read the letter, and she threw herself upon her knees.

"Why should she suffer and not I?" she cried, "and I am looking forward to happiness. Then she prayed long and fervently, not for happiness and blessings but for forgiveness!"

"I shall only be really happy when I know she has forgotten," she said to herself, and she knew that this meant when Sir Albert Gerald had won her sister.

The sun shone brightly on Grace's wedding-day. She was quiet and composed. When Lady Lyons praised her for her demeanour she said gravely,

"I am losing nothing, leaving no one, and I am gaining much."

The Duchess kissed her, and Lady Lyons moved forward a little. She had a vague idea she might be equally honoured, but was disappointed; however, there was the register signed by the Duke and Duchess, *that* would go down to posterity in connection with her son, and that was always a great deal.

As the small party left the church, they were met by Lady Penryn.

"Oh, you naughty girl!" she said, playfully. "You nice thing! where have you been all this time? Does she not look sweet?" appealing to the Duchess, who, passing on, took no notice of her.

She met with a cold reception from even Lady Lyons; but she was not to be daunted; laying a detaining hand on Grace's arm she said—

"The right thing for friends to know each other; the Duchess, my dear, introduce me."

"Let me introduce Mr. Lyons," said Grace, with much composure, and passed on to the carriage with Paul.

The discomfited lady received no comfort from her husband.

"If I had only known she was that sort of girl," she said, bitterly; "I always thought she was a nobody, and the Duchess gave her away!"

"Her father was most kind to my poor boy. I know nothing of his people, but he was a thorough gentleman. I never could understand why you would never take the slightest notice of the girl. However the thing's done now and cannot be mended."

He did not tell his wife that he had sent Grace a magnificent bracelet, and a kind and fatherly letter, offering to be of use to her.

She understood though he said nothing about his wife; and, avoiding all mention of Lady Penryn, she thanked him warmly, and told him about the Duchess and her kindness. Paul Lyons took his wife to Scotland, and to Inchbrae.

Grace saw for herself the clearness of the sea, the beauty of colouring—all the fitful charm which makes the Highlands so very lovely and so dear to its people.

"I think I know why you care for me," she said to Paul one day when they had been for a ramble, she on pony-back and he on foot beside her. "I understand, since I came here, how delightful it is never to know what to expect. I look out of my window in the morning and I see sunshine and blue sky, and a sea in which a thousand delicate colours melt and blend. Half-an-hour afterwards there are clouds, but all is still, light and the sun seem behind, and anxious to peep out again. Next comes darkness, the blue turns to indigo, the sea becomes grey and sullen. All is changed, and so it is ever new, and no one can ever be tired of it. Now, Paul, that is what I conceive to be my charm in your eyes; I am never quite the same, and therefore I hope you will never be tired of me!"

Margaret was in far better spirits, and looking so much more her old self, that Grace was happier about her; but not quite happy, she said to Paul,

"Till something happens which will happen——"

"And till that happens (which I know nothing about) I am to ask no questions?"

"You may ask hundreds—I shall answer none. Do you know, Paul, one thing in connection with our marriage weighed terribly on my mind, shall I tell you *that*?"

"Pray do, darling, unless it is something very uncomplimentary."

"I used to wonder what two people, bound to live together always, could ever find to talk about. I was so afraid I should find your conversation monotonous, and that I should not be able to rise to the occasion."

"I may tell you that long ago—before I knew you—I often wondered what married people could find to talk about all their lives; since I knew you I have only thought how delightful it would be to have you to talk to, all mine," said Paul simply.

Tears came into her eyes. "You are very good to me," she said; and then they went in.

To Mrs. Dorriman, Grace was "as nice as she could be," and the quartet were happy together, but the consequence of the old days left their trace in a certain constraint. Had Grace remained ill and lonely the kind little woman's heart would have gone out to her more, but she thought (as we often do think) that there was a certain injustice in Grace's being so happy, while Margaret, all for her (because of her impatient temper and other faults) was left to feel bitterly the consequences of a great mistake, entered into entirely from a false conception of what she owed her sister.

Margaret was forgetting, but there were many terrible moments to her. It is one of the many instances of that compensation which is the rule in life, in spite of all assertions to the contrary, that with a great gift—the great gift of poetry and imagination—comes often morbidness.

The high-strung note is oftenest the one that goes most out of tune; and the very vividness and gracefulness of fancy—that combination that makes a poet live in a world of his own—has often its darker side.

Margaret still, at times, lived through the old terrors, still fancied her child's voice called her. She was silent about these things. Every pang she suffered would be a remembrance to Grace. Grace, who was so softened and yet so bright, and who seemed to her to be so completely now the sister she had at one time imagined her to be.

Mrs. Macfarlane was always a friend they were glad to see, but it was Grace who spoke with satisfaction of their having no society, and perhaps nothing more thoroughly convinced Mrs. Dorriman how completely she was altered. They were not to stay long, those two; Paul had not very long leave of absence and wanted to get his wife south. Before they left, one day, Mrs. Dorriman, who had always that feeling about Margaret and the injustice of her suffering for Grace's fault, did want to say one word. She thought it was right, and she was resolved to do it.

"I am very glad you are happy, Grace," she began, the day before their departure.

"Thank you, auntie; you are very good to say so; I am very happy."

"It seems strange; of course we all know that whatever is, is right, but does it not seem strange that poor Margaret?..."

"What is strange about poor Margaret?"

"That you should be happy and that she ... should so suffer."

"Yes, every thing is strange in this world," Grace answered; "at least we think so."

"I am sure, sometimes, you must feel it all very much, though you look as though care and trouble had never touched you."

"Do you count that to me as a crime?" Grace asked in a peculiar tone.

"I sometimes wonder if you ever blame yourself." Mrs. Dorriman's tone was, for her, severe.

"I suppose we all do at times."

"Well, it seems hard."

"That we should blame ourselves?"

"You know I do not mean that."

"No," answered Grace very slowly, and looking at her with a sort of surprise in her face; "I know what all this means; you beat about the bush very badly, Mrs. Dorriman."

"Now I have offended you since you call me Mrs. Dorriman."

"You have offended me," said Grace, vehemently, "because you give me credit for being utterly heartless and cruel, and wanting in affection; you think that, because I am happy now, I have forgotten. I have forgotten nothing! I do blame myself! I know as well as you can tell me that my selfishness and impatience and everything else made Margaret wretched! Up till lately I was very very unhappy, and all her sufferings weighed upon me terribly, but now that I see happiness for her looming in the distance I do allow myself to be happy. It was not till I saw that quite clearly that I consented to marry Paul and to be happy myself!"

"Happiness for Margaret! I see nothing before her but the perpetual grief for her child."

"I see something more. She will always regret her child, but, though there is so much bitterness mixed up with the recollection of its death, she will learn to think more happily even about its loss. Has it never struck you that, had it lived, there must have been a horrible anxiety about it."

"She will never see it in that light."

"You are wrong, for last night I saw her reading something, and I saw it moved her strangely." Grace's own voice faltered for a moment; recovering herself quickly she said, "It was about the short-sightedness of mourning a loss too deeply and not reflecting that it was a veiled mercy, as it was often taken from the evil to come. We talked about it afterwards at night, and I know her thoughts, auntie, now."

"I hope you may be right," said Mrs. Dorriman, and let the conversation drop.

Grace thought she should never forget the night before, when she and Margaret had stood together in something of their old fashion. It had been wonderfully calm and still; the moon, so bright that they might have read by its light, was shining down upon the sea, turning its rippling surface to silver; the soft light, which yet makes such sharp, dark shadows, was on the hills. Every now and again came the curious little grumbling sound from below, where the waves lapped and splashed quietly against the rocks. These waves seemed held by a restraining hand, they were so quiet. A night-hawk gave its weird cry, and some owls hooted; the trees seemed to have nothing to say, their usual rustle was, for the time, stilled. The sisters, in their different ways, felt the great beauty of it all. Margaret had drawn closer to Grace, and the latter gave an affectionate caress. These nights touched a responsive chord in Margaret, that wonderful sympathy that exists between a poet and nature filled her heart to overflowing; and Grace, softened by the affection of her husband, a happier future to look forward to, was sufficiently enthusiastic to draw her out a little.

She began to talk of heaven and of her child.

"On such a night, Grace, there is undescribable peace, and yet these influences pass away and regrets press upon one."

"That is natural," said Grace, softly; "but I do sometimes feel that, in thinking of a little child, regrets must be softened to one. To leave the world before it has been tempted, before it has sinned, with the future in this world, the trials all unknown; you do not know, darling, what it may have been saved."

"You do not know how often that thought comforts me," said Margaret, very earnestly; "if it had lived there might have been perpetual dread of an hereditary curse. No, what troubles me now, in my sad moments, in those darker moods that I sometimes have to fight against, is my own self-reproach."

"And my own dear Margaret, if you suffer from self-reproach what must I do?" asked Grace, with the sincerest sorrow.

"Not about my marriage, Grace; wrong as it was, it brought its own retribution: but I reproach myself bitterly now for not having struggled against the position I was put into. Looking back now I cannot help seeing that there were many things I might have done. I was so afraid of my child being taken from me. I allowed that fear to paralyse my senses. I might have appealed to Mr. Sandford, and done many things I know now I might have done: and it would have been better for *him*; but I simply lived for my little one; my senses seemed numbed in all directions except in that one. I made it my idol; I prayed for it alone; I dreaded things for it; I worshipped it, and it was taken from me.... If only I knew that the little life had not been sacrificed to neglect I could remember it more happily; but in that fear lies the bitterness of my loss."

"Then you may remember it more happily," said Grace, feelingly, "because that London doctor said to me that the little child could not have been saved; there was something very delicate about it, and it had a very oddly-shaped head."

"Then I can say God is very good," said Margaret, so low that Grace could hardly hear her.

She began to talk again soon, about the scenery round them, and of Mrs. Dorriman.

"There is something—some dread she has. I have no idea what it is, but the curious thing is that she so entirely forgets at times; then something brings it before her again. I love her dearly, and I wish she was perfectly happy."

"I think she is a dear old thing," answered Grace; "but she always puts me in mind of some ivy or creeper that the wind has blown away from its support. She is one of the women who must have somebody to cling to, even if that somebody be tyranical and harsh like her brother."

"Yet, in his own way, he has been kind to us."

"Very much in his own way," said Grace, resentfully.

"I have a fancy about Mr. Sandford," Margaret said rather dreamily.

"You have generally nice fancies about most people, darling; tell your fancy to me."

"You will only laugh?"

"I swear not to laugh."

"You dislike him more than I do."

"I suppose I do, but do you know, Margaret, that since I am happier, I mean since I have had so much affection from my husband and not felt like a boat without oars or rudder, or whatever the thing is that steers it, I feel ever so much kinder about every body—even about him. I am quite convinced that if somebody left me a large fortune I should become a striking instance of overpowering amiability."

"It is a problem I never can solve. I often wonder whether trial or prosperity softens people best."

"It depends upon the material; nothing would hurt you; but for me, I am a sort of acid, and more acid makes me into an explosive."

"My fancy about Mr. Sandford is that at one time in his life, perhaps when he was quite young, he has suffered, and cruelly suffered, from some terrible injustice."

"Another case of acids mixing and blowing up," said Grace, laughing; "he is in a perpetual state of effervescence."

"No, but seriously, Grace, he has a great deal of good in him, and his devotion to his wife shows he has warm affections somewhere, and he has always been kind to me."

"You win every one, even Paul. I know well that you were his first grand passion, and curiously enough I am not jealous."

"Who talks of jealousy?" said a voice from below, and Paul, his cigar nearly ended, came under the window.

"I am merely saying, dear," said Grace in her most melting accents, "that, though you once were madly in love with Margaret, I am *not* jealous."

And laughing, Grace escaped to her own room. Margaret remained at the window. She was moved by what Grace had repeated to her about her child; yes, better to have lost it here than to have seen it that....

And Grace was really very happy. Paul was most kind and good, and there was more manliness about him now than she had ever thought him capable of; and yet, she said to herself, that for her to give her whole heart, to have such an affection for any one, such as Grace had for her husband, there must be higher qualities.

She must look up more, she must have help, and some one in whom she could find a better and a nobler self.

And in the softening influences of that hour and that scene a vivid blush rose to her face, and she told herself that already one was there; and that her heart, crushed as it had been, and cruelly as she had suffered, was not hopelessly embittered. She knew that she could love, and then she sighed. Large tears came into her eyes and rolled slowly down unchecked over her face, a sudden thrill of passion and of hope went through her frame, and she knew she did love!

Next morning came parting with Grace, but it was a parting in which she allowed no sorrow to appear.

She utterly bewildered Mrs. Dorriman by saying to her, "You will, I hope, soon have very good news to send me."

"About what, my dear?" and poor Mrs. Dorriman's face was expressive of blankest bewilderment.

"About every thing, generally," said Grace; "never mind about understanding now, you will some day; and it will be all right."

When she and Paul had waved a last farewell Mrs. Dorriman stood looking out of the window till the carriage became a speck upon the horizon.

"I wonder what Grace meant, Margaret my love? she does say such odd things, sometimes. Did you hear what she said to me just now?"

"I do not think I know which particular thing you mean, dear auntie; Grace says so many odd things."

"She hoped I should soon have very good news to send her. Now, my dear, what news can I have to send her from here? It really is a very odd saying and I am quite puzzled."

"Do not puzzle yourself; Grace often says things that have no meaning."

"But what do you think, Margaret? You know her so much better than I do. What are you thinking about, just now?"

"I am wondering if it is going to rain," Margaret said, and turned away laughing.

"As if I had spoken about the weather," the poor little woman said. But Margaret had left the room.

CHAPTER IX.

In these days unless adventures take the disagreeable form of accidents, nothing is likely to arise in a journey between the north of Scotland and the south of England to mar the serenity of one's temper.

Grace, carefully cherished all the way, travelled with supreme satisfaction. She saw in the distance, not very far off, happiness for Margaret. She grew more fond of her husband each day, in return for the affection he lavished upon her, and she had none of the anxieties to which she had once been no stranger.

There was but one cloud upon the horizon, and the one drawback to her perfect happiness lay in that fact. If it grew larger it might mar her happiness to a certain extent, and the fear that it might do so troubled her when she remembered it.

It may be recollected that neither Margaret or herself had conceived a very high opinion of Mr. Paul Lyons on first acquaintance; indeed, Margaret had had a good deal to do to bring herself to think happily about his being Grace's husband; then, on further acquaintance, she grew not only to like him but to recognise that there was much merit in the young man, and she was thankful her sister had fallen into such excellent and kindly hands.

Grace had been won by his affection for herself, and by the amount of admiration she inspired, but she did not take a very high view of his character, and that fact did not trouble her in the least. She always took exception to her sister's ideas as "high-flown," and, if she had been asked, would have answered that her husband aspired to nothing very great in the way of intellect or sentiment, but that he had quite enough for this work-a-day world, and more than enough for *her.* It was a daily surprise to her, therefore, to find that, even in little things, her husband had a very much higher standard than she had. This discovery was startling; she felt she must take care lest she forfeited his good opinion. Then one day he was talking about Margaret, and of her having divested herself of every farthing of her husband's money, and Grace laughed a little about it. She was astonished at the view he took of it; he was quite vehement about it.

"I cannot see it in your way," Grace had said. "It seems to me that, as poor Margaret married the man, she had every right to whatever he chose to leave her."

"I am sorry to hear you say that, even in fun (I know you are not in earnest). I should never have been able to think of Margaret in the same way if she had acted differently."

"But, Paul, *why*? Margaret suffered horribly and behaved like an angel. Why should she not reap any benefit?"

"It is not a thing to argue about, it is a thing one feels," he answered; "and I am quite grieved, darling, that you should pretend to think differently." This was pleasant; then Paul went on, "I cannot myself fathom her motives: but the way I read the story of her life is, that she was, for some reason, anxious to make a home for you—so you have told me—rushed into the scrape, and has repented ever since. Girls are so curious. I suppose she had the independence you have; so where the good of it all was I cannot see. Then, when she found what she had done, her better, higher nature prevailed, and she gave the money away."

"You really think it wrong to benefit in any way by that man's money?" asked Grace, horribly conscious, and feeling most uncomfortable; "supposing, Paul—only supposing—I had benefitted, would you have blamed me?"

"Do not put such absurd questions," he answered, sharply; "it is not the least like you to have done such a thing. Can you not see that, in one sense, in a sort of way, it is almost like blood-money? Imagine being the better for anything of the kind! I believe the money would bring a curse and not a blessing!"

Grace felt an acute and miserable pang of self-reproach; she was afraid now that her husband might find out, and she knew that the loss of his esteem would be terrible to her. He and Margaret thought so much alike; what could she do?

His appointment was worth a few hundreds a year, and the six hundred a year she had was counted in arranging their expenses.

Whenever the future was talked of, this miserable idea haunted her. When Paul advised her to get something, whenever money was in question, there was this one constant weight upon her mind, and the strange thing to herself was, that now she began to see a little as he did, and she could not now understand how she had reconciled herself to accepting it, how she could have claimed her right to this money so complacently.

Paul had proposed to her, thinking her penniless, and the small fortune had been a joyful surprise. How she wished now that she had never had anything to do with it!

But she could not see her way out of it. She knew that, if she spoke to Margaret, Margaret would do without things and help her, but for that very reason she could not speak to her.

Paul saw that his wife was not quite so bright as usual, but he thought she was tired, and was full of affectionate solicitude. Every attention he paid her, every kind word he uttered, gave her an additional pang.

They slept two nights on the journey, as Grace had always to be careful, and within an hour of London Mr. Stevens got into the carriage.

Grace saw him enter with some misgiving. The horrible thought occurred to her that perhaps he might refer in some way to investments or something that might lead her husband to make inquiry. She could only answer by speaking the truth. To her immense relief Paul said, "As you have some one to talk to now I will go and smoke," and so saying he left her with Mr. Stevens.

Grace felt now or never was her opportunity. Before Mr. Stevens could look round she poured out her trouble with a rapidity and vehemence that astonished him. When he, at length understood, he entered very fully into it all.

"Your husband is quite right; I should have the same feeling about it," he said.

"That makes it worse for me," said Grace, colouring, "but perhaps you have never had my temptation; you were never dependent upon others—very nearly penniless."

"Penniless, yes! Dependent, no!" he answered, "since I could work for my living."

"Mr. Sandford ruled my fate and Margaret's," answered Grace, "and that was never thought of; but I wish—oh! how I wish—I knew what to do. Would he help me?"

"Mr. Sandford is the one person who could help you," said Mr. Stevens; "a frank appeal to him might be productive of much good, and my advice to you is not to hide your trouble from your husband; let him know it; the fewer secrets between married people the less likely they are ever to disagree."

"I will tell him some day," answered Grace, "but I have behaved very badly to Mr. Sandford—he has no reason to love me."

"He is a man who has much to contend against, but he is a generous man. He never grudges money, and he can but say he can do nothing. I hope you left all well at Inchbrae," he said, with a resolute turning away from the subject.

"'*All*' consisting of Mrs. Dorriman and my sister," laughed Grace, rallying the moment her trouble was put out of sight.

"Ah! I am going there next week to meet Mr. Sandford; there is still something to be arranged between us."

"Then," asked Grace, "could you not say something for me? Could you not speak to Mr. Sandford for me?"

"I could, certainly, but Mr. Sandford dislikes me, and after all, to speak plain English, Mrs. Lyons, what can he do? There is only one way in which he can help you. If he chooses to pay you your income out of his own pocket, or to pay fifteen thousand pounds to your account. When you talk of help—which is an exceedingly vague word—you should put it in its practical form."

"Then everything is at an end," exclaimed Grace, and she leaned back upon the cushions in despair.

"I do not quite agree with you," he answered, "only I wished you to see the practical side of the question; there is no use in my going to a man like Mr. Sandford and when he puts the question, '*What does she expect me to do?*' have nothing to reply on your account."

"I cannot ask him to give me fifteen thousand pounds, it is impossible!" said Grace flushing at the curt tone used by Mr. Stevens.

"You need ask him for nothing; but help in this case means money—as it generally does; leave the sum to him, but you must understand when you use the world 'help' what it does mean. I merely wanted to prepare you for that."

"Thank you," said Grace, whose hopes were now sunk very low indeed.

She sat silent for a few moments, and then, looking up, said, "Supposing you spoke to Mrs. Dorriman, she can say many things to her brother no one else can, and she always understands."

"Yes," said Mr. Stevens in an odd tone, "I agree with you, she does understand most things."

"When do you go there?"

"On Thursday, I hope; and now, Mrs. Lyons, before we part let me know how am I to communicate with you."

"Can you write to me?"

"That is not quite impossible; but if your husband is to know nothing about this it seems to me that my writing to you upon business matters—now he is supposed to know all about your business—may lead to complications."

"You do not understand, Mr. Stevens, he—my husband—never asks any questions. I merely told him I had succeeded to fifteen thousand pounds; he was very much surprised and pleased, I suppose, but there the matter dropped. Mr. Sandford arranged all about the money matters for me, and the money was settled upon me and then upon my husband."

"That complicates matters of course; you have no power to give up money settled upon him; I see no way out of it."

"Do speak to Mrs. Dorriman," pleaded Grace, "she has a great opinion of you, and, if you put the matter before her, something might be done."

"I still advise you to tell your husband," said Mr. Stevens; "remember every day's delay makes confession more difficult afterwards. Then again, does not Lady Lyons know about it?"

"I do not think she does," but as she spoke Grace felt very uncomfortable. She once again entreated Mr. Stevens to speak to Mrs. Dorriman, and as Paul got into the carriage again she could only trust that her persuasion had been successful.

No one, however, can imagine how this dread of discovery weighed upon her. Each time Paul returned, when he had been out alone, her expression, when he appeared, was anxiety—did he know? had anything been said to make him suspicious?

"I am beginning to be afraid you are tired of me," he said one day; "when I come home now you never look the least pleased to see me."

"I am glad, dear; please do not take fancies into your head."

"Well, I wish you showed it a little more; I am longing to get you away—you are much less energetic than you were a little while ago. The way you stick to my mother is very unlike you. I am awfully fond of her, and all that, but I like having you a bit by myself, and her too for that matter."

Grace turned red and white by turns. She knew that she was suffering from irritability produced by anxiety. She was essentially one who could stand neither fatigue of body nor anxiety of mind.

"What can you have to say to your mother that I may not hear?" she asked, with a certain sharpness of tone that surprised him. He looked at her attentively, and that seemed to displease her still more. To his unbounded astonishment she burst out crying, and cried with a sort of miserable, helpless vehemence, that was infinitely distressing to him.

"My darling! can you not tell me what is wrong?" he said, "for there *is* something wrong, you are not yourself. Who can you turn to if you have any worry or distress so well as to your husband? Have you no confidence in me?"

"Don't," she sobbed, "you only make me worse!"

He was deeply wounded, not so much by her words as by the way she shrank from him.

Lady Lyons made her voice heard in the passage, asking if her son was in, and Grace snatched her hand from Paul, and rushed out of the room by one door as her mother-in-law came in at the other.

Paul was an affectionate son, but at that particular moment he would have preferred to have had time to discover what was the matter with his wife, and he was so absorbed that his mother told him a fact very interesting to her, and which she considered should have been equally interesting to him, without his taking it in.

"My *dear* Paul," she said at length, "you are not attending to me one bit!"

"I beg your pardon, mother, I think I heard what you said."

"About the doctor, Paul?"

"I think so," he answered, trying to recall her words.

"Well, you see, I shall have to get another that being the case."

"A very good thing, I should say."

"Paul! the death of an eminent medical man is not a subject for rejoicing."

"Oh! he is dead. Who is dead, mother?"

"Dr. Dickson, and you said you heard what I said. Oh! Paul."

"Well, I hear now, and I do not think I ever heard Doctor Dickson's name before."

"After that!" said Lady Lyons, throwing up her hands; "he was the only man—the only man who quite understood my constitution."

"Well, I'm sorry he is dead if he was useful to you, mother, but you have been no better and no worse ever since I can remember anything. Would you mind my leaving you for a moment? I am afraid Grace is not well."

He left her and went to find his wife.

Grace had recovered herself, and reproached him for making "a fuss."

"You know I am not strong," she said, "and easily sent up and down. I am like a shuttlecock, and sometimes, Paul, I feel that we are not as much alike as we thought."

"Now you have hurt and vexed me still more," he said, in a tone of real vexation. "What discoveries will you make next? In what way am I your inferior? I know in many ways I am, but in what particular am I wanting to-day?"

"My inferior!" said Grace, with sudden passion; "I feel beneath you in all things—in principle, in every thing."

She covered her face with her hands.

"I cannot understand you, dear," he said, kindly; "and if you do not wish to tell what all this means leave it alone. But my hope was that you had learned to confide in me, and I am disappointed. My mother is there, do as you like about seeing her. I said you were not well."

"I am all right," she said, throwing off her depression and her penitence at once. "Go to your mother, Paul; I am sorry you said anything about my not being well, it was only a passing indisposition."

He left her not fully satisfied, but knowing it was useless to press her further.

Lady Lyons was overflowing with motherly sympathy, and fussed in a way Grace thought nearly intolerable, and which in days not so very long ago she would have ungraciously put a stop to.

But Paul's mother was to her a different person from the Lady Lyons she had known and laughed at in the old days, and she bore her attentions with all possible patience.

The trio sat down to dinner with those subdued feelings generally indicative of a past storm.

Lady Lyons resented Paul's evident want of interest in her physicians; and Grace was exhausted, and annoyed with herself for having given way as she had done; while Paul, while trying to converse with his mother, was conscious of a painful impression about his wife which he could not shake off.

The atmosphere was therefore not very clear to begin with; and poor Lady Lyons, feeling that subtle constraint that somehow had arisen between husband and wife, threw all at once an explosive just when Grace was least expecting it.

"It will interest you to hear, my dear, that before I came up here I went to see the grave of your little niece. I found it well-cared for, flowers, and all that you know."

"It does not interest me much," answered Grace, very languidly. "I never saw the poor little thing, and everything connected with that time is so hateful to me I never willingly recall it."

"As things are, is that not a little ungrateful, my dear? And he deserves your gratitude—poor Mr. Drayton!"

"What has Grace got to be grateful for to that unhappy man?" asked Paul, with very faint curiosity.

"The money, my dear, the fortune; surely you know?"

"I hold my money from my sister," said Grace, defiantly.

"Ah! but, my dear, if he had not left it to your sister she could not have given it to you!" said Lady Lyons, quite sure now that she had put the case convincingly.

Grace grew as white as marble; she did not dare look at Paul. Rallying all her power, she said—

"It makes a great difference taking money from my sister and taking it from Mr. Drayton."

"I see no difference," said Paul, in a cold hard tone she had not believed him capable of.

"There!" said Lady Lyons. "Paul will perhaps convince you—since that money came to you...."

"Do leave the subject alone, Lady Lyons—it is hateful to me!"

"Why, dear me, my dear, this is only a whim. I am quite sure Paul agrees with me."

"I hate the subject also," said Paul angrily; and poor Lady Lyons, utterly unconscious of how she had managed to make things unpleasant, saw she had done so and began to apologise.

But Paul's expression, the disgust she saw written in his face, was too much for Grace, worn out as she was with the anxiety this very subject had given her, and she rose, tried to move to the door, and fell into her husband's arms in a faint—out of which they found it difficult to rouse her.

Paul was sorry for her and very anxious. He had seen her suffer, but he had never known her faint like this before.

For the moment, and till she recovered, everything was forgotten; but when she came round again Grace saw that she had fallen in her husband's eyes, and cried bitter tears when he turned away.

Yes, she had fallen. How often occasions had arisen when he might have been told the truth! How utterly she had kept him in the dark! He was resentful, and it was not in him to see any circumstances in extenuation. If she thought it right to benefit by this man's money, why not have said so frankly? In any conversation about Margaret, when he had spoken his mind, what was there to prevent her saying what the case was?

Mingled with indignation at the way he had been treated was also the bitter fact that they would be so much poorer than he had imagined, because, of course, the money should go back. It was the price of Margaret's happiness, and he would have none of it.

Lady Lyons, with the best intentions, drove him nearly wild that evening.

It is wonderful what powers of irritation very well-meaning people possess when they are endowed with blunt perceptions and limited intelligence.

Some days passed on. There was constant constraint between the two who, up till now, had been so happy. Then there came the day before they sailed.

Grace was lying back in a chair, looking pale and weary, and her husband was writing.

All at once he looked up and said briefly—

"Grace, that money must be given up."

"Yes," she said, and he thought he heard a little sob.

"How you can care to keep it!" he said, trying to subdue his feelings because she was evidently so unwell.

"I care to keep it! If you only knew how I hate myself for ever having cared! Paul, do you remember your being so violent—speaking so strongly about it. It took away my courage. I could not tell you, and it has been making me so wretched!"

"But why was I kept in the dark about it from the first?" he asked, always trying to control himself. "Why was it talked of as a legacy?"

"There was no reason you should not have known at first. I described it to your mother as a legacy (it was, in the first instance, left to Margaret); it saved explanations, and I did not care for her to know. You never inquired how the money had come to me. If you had asked one direct question, I should have been forced to speak the truth to you."

"I see no difference," he said again.

He was most terribly annoyed; the whole thing was a shock to him, and he was all the more annoyed because he was conscious that the increase to his income had been pleasant, and that it had helped to smooth their path so much.

Without it how could he afford Grace's extravagant habits? He knew that the money coming from his own appointment was not enough, and out of that even he had given his mother something. If he now explained to her how could he explain without hurting his wife and showing that perfect confidence had not existed between them?

In spite of all these considerations he never for one moment thought of retaining the money. To him it was the price of Margaret's happiness, and he now turned over in his mind how he could say something to his mother without entering into details which would be so painful to him.

He turned away once more from his wife, and once again he said, as he had said before,

"The money must go back."

Grace was very miserable. She had learnt to love her husband and to find much to help her in his directness, and a certain strength she had not expected to find in his character. When she had married him she had thought that in all important things she would be the guiding star. He was slow in thought, and she valued her own quickness over-much; that position of being a sort of "Triton among minnows" at a second-class school influenced her fatally still, and to fall, as she had fallen, was a bitter mortification to her. She sat down now to write to Margaret, and, as she wrote and repeated her husband's sentiments, she began herself to see things more as he did.

In the meantime poor Paul had a very difficult task before him. He had to make his mother understand, without explanations, that his promise of help, as far as a regular increase to her income went, could not be carried out.

Lady Lyons heard with dismay, in which a certain irritation against him for having raised false hopes was plainly visible.

"I have engaged a footman," she said, helplessly; "and now I must send him away. It will look so odd."

"I am very sorry."

"It would have been different, of course, if you had said nothing about it: then, you quite understand, Paul, that *then* I could have had nothing to complain of."

Paul did quite understand. He went out as soon as he could, going to his club and entering it with that sense of leaving domestic and other troubles behind him which makes club-land enviable to those who know it not.

But the remembrance of his lessened resources came before him there. A friend asked him to give his subscription to help the family of a mutual friend. Paul was obliged to say, with great reluctance, that he found, on reconsideration, he could not do it. This was doubly hard, as, with the full consciousness of a good balance in the bank, he had himself originated the idea.

A clever man would simply have stated the fact of finding himself less well off than he expected, and the fact so stated would have been held sufficient excuse; but Paul Lyons was not clever, and he hesitated, muttered something about not being his own, and gave his friends directly an unfavourable impression.

Manner so often speaks more plainly than words.

Even this refuge seemed to have lost its charm now this unexpected annoyance had crept up.

He could himself do nothing to strip himself of this money since it was not his but belonged to his wife. He took a long walk by the Embankment, and, in the mood he was in, it was natural that the past, with all its follies and the many foolish and wrong things he had done when he was younger, came before him. What right had he to judge his wife so severely? His temptations and hers were different; was his standard so much higher than hers because he had not known the want of money as she had? He began to feel that he had behaved unkindly, and hurried back to that hotel in Brook Street where they were again staying. He would apologise, and, though he could not keep that money, and hoped she would give it up, still they had enough to get on with;—if their bread had no butter, still, there would be bread.

He arrived tired out, and was confronted by his mother, in a state of abject despair, her face blurred with tears, who announced that Grace had gone!

What had passed? It was in vain that he tried to get Lady Lyons to tell him, in rational order, anything about his wife's departure.

Afraid of her son's anger, bewildered by Grace's sudden departure, the poor lady's ideas were entangled in a confusion from which she could not extricate herself; and her son, accustomed as he was to sift her statements, could make nothing of them now. Suddenly she quoted something said by Sir Albert Gerald.

"Was he here then?"

"Yes, he was here. I think, Paul, though I am not quite sure, and I do not want to assert anything not quite the case, that Grace sent for him."

Paul had a natural movement of anger;—Why should a third person be sent for by his wife? What business had any third person to come between them?

"Where has she gone?" he asked, his self-reproach of an hour ago still softening him towards Grace.

"I really do not know—but to Scotland I think. I heard her say to Sir Albert, 'You will escort me,' and he said he was going to Scotland, so I suppose she has gone there also."

"And left no message, or note, or anything for me?" said Paul, with rising anger, not yet fully understanding that Grace had really gone.

"Oh, my dear Paul! how stupid I am. Yes, she left a note for you, or a letter—let me see was it a letter?—no, I remember thinking it was oddly folded."

"Will you please give it to me?" asked Paul with the calmness of despair.

"My dear Paul, if you would only not hurry me and flurry me so," said his mother, as she sought in her pockets, one after another, and then looked under the china ornaments on the mantel-piece, and drove her son wild altogether.

At last she said as a brilliant idea crossed her mind, "I remember now. I was so afraid of forgetting it that I put it inside one of your slippers, Paul, and I knew that you were quite sure to find it to-night, when you put your slippers on. I think it was rather clever of me, eh Paul?"

But Paul had left the room.

As he read his wife's note, consisting only of a few lines, he felt he loved her very dearly. She had gone to Richmond, she could not bear to see him so changed towards her.

"When you have forgiven me, if you can forgive me, then I will come back," she said.

Paul knew he had forgiven her, but he was still sore about that third person intervening. He was on his way to Richmond before many minutes were over.

Grace received him with intense satisfaction, she was ready to promise everything. Then came that question about Sir Albert Gerald.

"Is it possible you do not really understand all that story?" asked Grace, who, now, with that weight removed from her mind, and restored to her husband's affection, was in tremendous spirits.

"I understand nothing about him. What story do you mean?"

Then his wife enlightened him.

"I was to let him know about Margaret when I thought it would not hurt his cause—I was to send for him."

"Oh!" said Paul, "then you think he is in love with Margaret?"

"I do not think it, I know," she answered, laughing.

That evening dinner was ready at the Brook Street Hotel—three covers were laid.

"I think you may remove one cover," said Lady Lyons, "only two are going to dine to-night."

The waiter looked surprised and hesitated, then the door opened, and Grace, beaming, entered, followed by Paul.

CHAPTER X.

Mrs. Dorriman was not a little perplexed just then by the delay in her brother's arrival. She had lost much of her dread in connection with those papers which had at one time weighed so heavily upon her, and the affection which had sprung up between her and her roughly-spoken brother made her feeling in regard to a possible fault he might have committed sink into the background. But all through her little daily duties, rendered sweeter and pleasanter because of Margaret's companionship, when she was reading or working, walking by the burn-side, or gliding along on the sea in a boat, whatever her occupation was there was a subtle indefinable consciousness of something impending, which did not actually make her unhappy, but which kept her in a state of suppressed mental excitement.

Mr. Stevens had something to do with her not dwelling upon this coming explanation unduly. He seemed to be ubiquitous, flying here and there and everywhere at one and the same moment. He seemed to think so little of what he called running up to London, but he managed to spend a great deal of his time at Inchbrae.

There was a great deal he consulted Margaret about, but she was quick enough to see that business was not always the real reason of his visits. It often happened that a letter might have done just as well, and nothing but a dread of seeming inhospitable, made Margaret refrain from saying so.

Margaret was so accustomed to find that without any effort on her part those few specimens of mankind she had met always managed to fall in love with her, that she was afraid now of this being the case, and she puzzled Mr. Stevens by becoming all at once distant and reserved with him—her manner became changed and cold.

It was only natural that she should become her own heroine, now she had no Grace to think of, and that all interest centred in herself.

Mrs. Dorriman spoiled and petted her. Jean thought her perfection; the people liked her manner, which was both gentle and courteous to them; and when they discovered that she was a "giving" lady their respect and affection rose to enthusiasm. The few outsiders knew that she had faced a tragedy; and the death of her child, her husband's insanity, everything combined to surround her with the halo of suffering, which sets a woman apart from other women.

There was little in the surroundings of Inchbrae to draw out her sympathies. The people were not badly off, the crofter question had not cropped up, and the soil was fertile. Now and again a sick woman wanted soup and she got it, or a child was in need of some garment which gave occupation, but this was all.

Margaret was essentially a loveable woman, and had that air of dependence which (though frequently misleading enough) appeals so forcibly to the chivalrous side of mankind, and, with the claim it establishes, so often creates, an affection besides.

She was what people call sentimental, but not in the mis-used sense of that very ill-used word. Just as the commonest objects in life, a broken bough, a shallow pool, the faded leaf upon the grass, resolve themselves into pictures to the eye of an artist, so where the poetic faculty exists (more especially when it has been developed by suffering) all the various incidents of life, all the impulses and influences of personal life, become unwritten poems. Margaret had suffered terribly; the suffering was healing under the influence of time, but leaving a vivid imagination. She lived much over again, she dwelt morbidly upon her own shortcomings, and she began to be dangerously near an all-absorbing selfishness.

There was one pleasure that never palled upon her—the effect of natural beauty is so different upon different temperaments. The freshness of a sea-bound coast, the tints of grey and green, the harmony of all, is felt by some who recognise the quickened circulation, and call it health-giving; and so it is.

To a poet, however, this harmony of nature says something more—there is a deeper and fuller meaning in it all, whether the faculty of expression be given or not. Heaven and earth do not seem far apart when the soul is stirred to its very depths. The secret of those forces that carry awe when manifested in their grandest power, has a key-note, which, begun here, is carried upwards. Margaret had the power of expression, and her poems became to her the best and highest part of her life; she no longer cared to publish them; so much of herself was in them that she shrank from letting any one read them. She lived in a world of her own, a world full of beauty, but one in which self entered too much.

Grace's letter, with its violent expressions of remorse, and its incoherent account of having left Paul, broke in upon her self-absorbed feelings with rather a rude shock.

She knew Grace too well to doubt the despair of which her sister wrote, as though it and remorse henceforward were to be her portion; but she could not doubt her sincerity about the money; the cry was too natural, and Margaret's own sentiments were in such complete accordance with it.

It had been painful to her the ease with which Grace had accepted the money, and she felt thankful now that they had this point in common.

In her own mind the argument she had used seemed conclusive. "I vowed a vow I could not keep, and the benefit arising from a broken vow cannot justly be mine."

She rose to answer this letter, which had disturbed her, and, opening the door, found Mr. Stevens just coming into the hall.

"Can you spare me a moment?" he said, with some anxiety.

She answered "Yes," trusting that his business was really business.

"I have had such an extraordinary letter from Mr. Sandford," he began. "I wrote to him about money matters, and his answer is, that he is not in a position to advance a penny anywhere. I am afraid things have gone very wrong; have you heard anything?"

"Nothing to this effect. Mrs. Dorriman cannot imagine why he does not come."

"He says, '*I am utterly penniless, and can do nothing!*' It is most extraordinary!"

"I wonder if Mrs. Dorriman knows anything? shall I go and find her?"

"No; I have written to Mr. Sandford for an explanation; till I hear again there is no use making her unhappy."

"It will affect her?" Margaret asked, with real interest.

"It will affect her. She told me once she had no settlements, and was entirely dependent upon her brother."

"I am so grieved."

"It will, of course, affect you also, Mrs. Drayton. It seems very hard upon both of you."

"And my sister is giving up that money; Paul Lyons cannot bear her having it."

"I have made up my mind. I am going to ask you a great favour, Mrs. Drayton."

"Pray do not," said Margaret, much distressed, and turning rosy red.

"Why?" he asked, astonished, and very much offended with her.

"We had better ... do let us remain friends," she said, pleadingly.

"What else do I want?" he asked, very much astonished at her changing colour.

"Oh," said Margaret, drawing a long breath and speaking with evident relief; "of course I will do anything for you."

He looked suspiciously at her.

"You young ladies are so cautious in these days; you answered as though I was going to ask you to lend me ten thousand pounds, or lay a proposal of marriage at your feet."

Again Margaret coloured violently, but she laughed also; she felt she had so nearly made herself supremely ridiculous.

"What I want you to do," continued Mr. Stevens, earnestly, "is nothing very remarkable. I want you to manage that I shall have a little time alone with Mrs. Dorriman. I have something to say to her, and it so happens that I never can see her alone; you are always there, you know."

How Margaret laughed to herself!

"My dear Mr. Stevens," she said, all the former charm and cordiality of her manner once again in full force, "how dreadfully sorry I am that I have been so blind and so stupid. I am afraid I have been dreadfully in your way."

"Well, you have rather," said Mr. Stevens, who was disappointed to find her manner, capricious; he had thought her above that sort of thing.

Margaret laughed again, but she went upstairs, put on her things, and then found Mrs. Dorriman, who was still weighing in her own mind the respective merits of cranberry or blackberry jam for the pudding that evening.

"Which does Mr. Stevens like best? for I think he will dine here to-night," Margaret said, with a smile the little lady did not understand.

"Have you asked him, my dear?" she asked placidly; "I did not know he was here."

"No, but I think you will ask him. He is here, and, by the way, he wants to see you about something."

Mrs. Dorriman took off her housekeeping apron, washed her hands, and went composedly to meet her fate, with an innocence and want of suspicion that gave Margaret much quiet amusement.

Mrs. Dorriman was a little nervous, because she thought perhaps Mr. Stevens brought her news from her brother. She had not heard from him for some days, and she expected him daily; since the frequent attacks of illness, which she did not thoroughly understand the import of, a vague uneasiness filled her.

"Is my brother well? Have you news of him?" she asked hastily, when she went into the room.

"He was well enough when I heard," he answered; and then a sudden shyness possessed him.

She waited for him to speak, and he noted, with much admiration, that when she sat expectant she did not fidget. This power of stillness he counted a great merit. Nothing annoyed him so much as being spoken to in turns, with an intense and unflattering attention towards an uninteresting piece of work, or what he considered uninteresting.

"I wish," he said suddenly, "that you could think of some one else as much as you do of your brother!"

Startled, she raised her eyes, and his look confused her.

"I——I have no one else," she said, in a low voice.

"Yes, you have, Mrs. Dorriman, if only you will try to think so. I believe—I am afraid the idea is new to you—but could you not try and like me a little? I cannot tell you how I have learned to love you! but you are so good and so unselfish. I think—I am quite sure—there is nobody like you!..."

Margaret, sitting on the stone seat, heard voices coming towards her. She rose, and went to meet those two who, after the flush of youth and bloom was passed, had for the very first time found a real home in the heart of another.

Mrs. Dorriman seemed to have renewed her youth; the flush in her face, and the serenity of her brow, made her look so much younger.

She walked as in a dream. She had for so long now thought of Mr. Stevens as a most kind and most helpful friend; and she had always admired that independence and straight-forwardness that upheld the right without roughness. And this man loved her! How wonderful, she thought in her humility, how extraordinary, that he, with the whole world to choose from, should love *her*—wish her to be his wife.

Margaret's congratulations were most heartfelt. She understood the charm to Mr. Stevens that lay in Mrs. Dorriman's sweetness and gentleness, and there was something frank and pleasant about him.

The sight of these two, so utterly and quietly happy, did make her think a little of the emptiness of her own life; but she would not dwell upon this—she would try and throw her energies into some useful direction. In the meantime, she would do her utmost not to mar Mrs. Dorriman's happiness by any repinings about leaving Inchbrae. The place was very dear to her; she had grown to love it; but she knew that there was no scope here for her energies. She must turn her steps southwards; she would not make a third in the little household. Perhaps Mr. Sandford might wish her to remain with him, and she would do this. She told herself she would do whatever was really right.

Mr. Stevens, before he left Inchbrae, made Anne Dorriman give him a solemn promise—a promise that she gave him smiling till, she saw him grave.

"Promise me, Anne, that, come ill or good fortune, nothing will turn you from marrying me!"

"I promise."

She said it thoughtfully, and then insisted on his repeating the words.

"Now," he said, "if every shilling of your brother's has gone, if you are left without one, still you will be my wife?"

"You are speaking as though you knew," she said, looking at him inquiringly; but he turned her words aside, and she forgot them.

"What have I done to deserve this happiness?" she asked of Margaret later, when the two went to their rooms.

"Much," said Margaret, gently. "Have you ever lived for yourself?—never since I knew you! I was thinking only to-day that it was not good for me to be with you, because you make so much of me and so little of yourself, that I am growing narrow and selfish."

"Nonsense! my dear," answered Mrs. Dorriman. "Oh! Margaret, if you knew how I hate being alone and having to decide things myself—now think of the comfort of having some one to go to!"

"And so able to help you," said Margaret, feelingly.

She also felt this burden of loneliness; felt it all the more because of the contrast between her own life and that of others.

Christie was much moved when the news was told her.

"It is coming near, my dear," she said to Margaret, "in the Lord's good time."

Margaret did not comprehend her.

Jean was most amusing upon the subject.

"And what for no!" she asked, when Mrs. Dorriman told her. "You have never had real true love, though Mr. Dorriman, poor man, was aye fond of you in his way; but he was a crookit stick, with no pith in him. This man's a man to be proud of. There's stuff in him, and you will be able to lean on him. It's not a light puff of wind will blow him down!"

Mrs. Dorriman wrote to her brother, and, in a few words which she found difficult to write, told him of her engagement.

She also said that she trusted Margaret would fill her place and live with him. "I think Margaret will be more to you than I could ever be." She wound up by saying, "You have been kind, but I have always felt that you were disappointed in me. I am not strong-minded enough to be a good companion for one so accustomed to more intelligence."

Had she deliberately steeped her pen in gall she could not have given him a bitterer moment.

He was physically unfit for any excitement or worry. His illness had gained rapidly upon him, and he suffered terribly at times.

He received a letter from Margaret which also troubled him greatly.

Knowing him to be well off, and that he did not care about money for its own sake, she wrote with confidence to him about Grace.

"She has given up the money left to her after me which I refused to take. I am afraid that giving it up will embarrass her and Paul. You have often offered to settle money upon me—to give me much that I did not want—will you do something for my sister? will you arrange something to make up to her for what she has given up? I think you feel with me, that accepting that money would humiliate me whether it was accepted by Grace or by myself."

A few days and then came the answer.

> "DEAR MARGARET,
>
> "I have nothing to give. I have no right to give anything, and I have not got it in my power. I am ill, and I am miserable. When I can I am going to Inchbrae. I have something to say to my sister. I think your ideas about that overstrained."

To say Margaret was disappointed is to say little. She doubted now whether the stand she had taken was the right one. All at once she seemed to see everything differently; for a moment or two she felt as though her sensitiveness on this subject had led Grace to disaster.

But, on re-reading her sister's letter, she saw that her objections had had no weight; it was Paul who thought as she did; it was because of her husband that Grace had yielded.

Before she had time to arrange in her own mind whether it would be wise or not to let Mrs. Dorriman know about Mr. Sandford's illness and his loss of fortune, Mrs. Dorriman had come up to her and recognised her brother's writing.

At first when Margaret tried to put her off with the convenient word "business," Mrs. Dorriman was ready to believe it, but Margaret's countenance was expressive; and the little woman, anxious at any rate about her brother, got so hysterical that she was only pacified by its being given her.

"I must go to him!" she exclaimed as she saw the tremulous handwriting; "he must be very ill."

"You had better ask Mr. Stevens what he thinks," said Margaret, gently.

"My dear, yes. What a comfort it is to have some one with a good head on his shoulders who will advise me what is best to be done. It is such a comfort! But I am very unhappy about my brother; I must write at once."

"Why not telegraph? Mr. Stevens lives near Renton; if you telegraphed and asked him to find out if your brother is seriously ill, and if he advises you to go to him, you would have the answer much sooner. We might easily drive in ourselves with the telegram and wait for the answer, or go and wait at Mrs. Macfarlane's."

"My dear Margaret, what a practical person you are; and I know exactly where Mr. Stevens is just now. He told me how he mapped out his day, and at this moment he is in the counting-house at Renton, and will be there till three."

"Then we will lose no time," said Margaret.

They had long ago invested in a pony and pony-carriage of their own, and were soon speeding on their way, Mrs. Dorriman thoughtful and anxious, sustained by a consciousness of that help she had so recently become possessed of; Margaret silent, wondering a little what her life was really going to be, noticing, with a little pang, that even Mr. Sandford, lonely and suffering though he was, said not one single word about her going to him.

Something in the scenery brought Sir Albert Gerald to her mind. She wondered if he ever thought of her now; it seemed strange that he had dropped so completely out of her acquaintance—for months she had heard nothing of him. More than once she had said something about him in her letters to Grace, but she never took any notice, evidently, thought Margaret, not understanding how much she was interested in him as a friend, since it was only natural after what had passed between them. She seemed to herself to have missed happiness all through her life. Had either her father or mother lived, or had she understood what Sir Albert meant about being free? Where was the use of this going back to old regrets? She blamed herself because she had thought he would, before now, have made some sign. After all, there were many other girls in the world, and no one could have had so sad a history; she had no right to be disappointed, and yet she knew she was bitterly disappointed.

They went straight to the little post-office, and, while Mrs. Dorriman despatched the telegram, Margaret sent the pony to the inn-stables, and then went to ask for letters.

There was one from Grace. After dwelling rapturously upon a new cloak, which, she said, she should call charity, because it covered so many sins in the shape of old-fashioned garments, telling of a bonnet she had fallen in love with and could not afford, recounting trifling adventures that had befallen her, she said,

"Do you know of any grand passion Sir Albert is likely to have? I hear he has left London to go and offer himself, his fastidiousness, his fine place, and his treacherous heart, to some one he has long secretly loved. I cannot help feeling angry because, because, because.... I hoped some one I knew had attracted him. Pray do not swear at me or say anything disagreeable, but it is horrid: and I think men are a mistake generally, always excepting, of course, Paul, with the biggest P you can imagine, and I am not sure I would say that did I not feel that he may look over my letter."

A great weight settled upon poor Margaret's spirits. This was the solution she had feared, and yet how far more painful is the story told by a friend than the one we tell ourselves. The world suddenly became dark to her; she was conscious of Mrs. Dorriman's joy and satisfaction on receiving Mr. Stevens's telegram. Her brother was better, but would like them both to go to him towards the end of the week. "You cannot possibly make the troublesome journey alone, but I will go for you and Mrs. Drayton," was the substance of his telegram, and the poor little woman remembered vividly how, with far less experience, she had had to make this very journey alone, and how she felt forlorn and unhappy and received no comfort from any one.

They lunched with Mrs. Macfarlane, who was delighted Mrs. Dorriman was going to have such a nice husband. She was in such good spirits, so cheerful, and so overflowing with prosperity, that poor Margaret felt her, for the first time, oppressive. She exerted herself on the way home to enter into Mrs. Dorriman's satisfaction, but every word uttered in most innocent self-gratulation gave her companion an additional pang.

"To be so cared for, for the first time in all my life! Not possible to make that troublesome journey alone! What have I done, Margaret, to deserve it all? How can I be thankful enough?"

The afternoon was still only half over when they got home to Inchbrae. The day's brightness was as yet undimmed, and yet on the far-off hills lay soft shadows. The sun was capricious as a youthful beauty, now shining in all its glory and turning the rippling sea to gold, and then veiling himself behind those fleecy clouds that floated over the various peaks and crags. Margaret, throwing off the bonnet she only wore when she made expeditions to the little town, went bareheaded down the burn-side, anxious to face out her trouble and fight that battle with herself which her sister's letter rendered necessary.

The influences of such an afternoon should by rights have soothed her. A temperament such as hers, keenly susceptible as it was, should have become more in harmony with the glowing, peaceful, and brilliant scene around. But when the soul is deeply wounded the very fairness and serenity of lovely scenery jars upon it, and the cry is akin to one bereaved who has lost its all here, and feels the day garish and the sunshine a mockery.

There was that ever-trembling whisper of the burn, that sounded not long ago to her telling her a love story. Now she would have given worlds to stop it since it told her lies. Everything, she thought, was happy but herself; the very bees had a heartless hum as they rejoiced over a bed of golden crowsfoot and wild thyme close at hand; and when from a little fishing-boat came a cheery Gaelic song, cheery and yet melancholy because of its minor key, Margaret's self-restraint gave way, and, covering her face with her hands, she cried quietly, but quite heart-brokenly.

On the hill-side came a rapid footstep, that yet was not heard on the short, well-nibbled grass; a few hill-sheep raised their heads and looked with a certain wonder at the intruder, not moving a step, since they knew no fear. Margaret only heard the slight rustle, when some one stood close to her; she had not time to wipe away her tears; startled, she rose, and there calling her softly, and with outstretched hands, was Sir Albert Gerald.

"What has distressed you?" he said, noting with quick sympathy her tearful face.

How could she tell him? He was here, and the look in his eyes, the whole expression of his face, told her that he had come to seek *her.* Grace's story was true, why had she made herself miserable? How stupid she was! Blushing, she answered part of his question, and he was content.

"I thought that you would never come again."

What change had come over everything?

Margaret thought the day brighter, softer, more enchanting than ever before known. She moved as in a dream, outwardly quiet, a whole world of passion, and love, and gratitude, swelling her heart.

"I am afraid of my happiness," she said that evening to Mrs. Dorriman, when Sir Albert had gone out with his cigar, and the two friends had gone upstairs to bed. "I am so intensely, so perfectly, happy! God is very good to me!"

"My dear," said Mrs. Dorriman, "I am nearly as happy about you as I am about myself, and I think Mr. Stevens is right (he is always right). He says we need not question why we are happy, but enjoy it, and be thankful for it. I like Sir Albert very much indeed, and if he cannot quite compare with ... older men just now, I dare say when he comes to be older——"

"He will be a second Mr. Stevens," said Margaret, laughing, as she said good-night.

Next day brought Mrs. Dorriman a letter from her brother, the contents of which puzzled her and bewildered her very nearly as much as the famous letter had done more than two years and a half ago, when we first made her acquaintance.

She was to come to Renton with Margaret, and she was also to bring Christie with her. Jean of course would be welcome, but he wished to see Christie particularly.

Mr. Stevens not having arrived, Mrs. Dorriman took her perplexities to Margaret.

"Why he should want to see Christie is so very remarkable," said she, in something of the old puzzled and plaintive tone.

"Did he know her in old days?"

"Of course he must have seen her, as a young man he must have known her, because she lived on the place, and it was our way to know everybody; but all these years she has been here and he has never taken any notice of her. I believe she would hardly know him by sight now."

"Perhaps she is connected with some memory of his youth."

"Yes! of course that may be it."

Mrs. Dorriman went herself to tell Christie about it; wishing to prepare the old woman, doubtful as to her consenting to go on a railway for the first time in all her life.

But when she reached Christie's cottage she found her in her Sunday's clothes—her best mutch[1] on, and all the small possessions she wished to take with her ready packed.

"How did you know, Christie?" she asked in great amazement.

"When I heard Mr. Sandford was ill and not likely to mend, I wanted to go and see him. I made ready; I have something to say to him, for your sake, my dear!"

Mrs. Dorriman sat down to rest.

"For my sake!" she repeated. "Oh! Christie, I want nothing from him."

"But I do for you, and for myself I would die in the old place; for you, I'd best keep quiet a bit longer."

She said no more of her hopes and wishes, but her parting words were:

"When you're ready I'm ready; not but what railways are fearful things to be sent about the world, with nothing but a screech and a puff of smoke."

Mr. Stevens in the meantime entered into various details with Mrs. Dorriman, even helping her to settle what things she would take with her or leave behind.

"There is one thing you must take, as Sandford expressly wishes you to do so." He spoke looking at her a little curiously.

A flash of recollection came to her.

"The box and papers," she exclaimed.

"*A* box and papers. Never again shall I say that all women are full of curiosity! I know differently now."

"You know everything, I think," said Mrs. Dorriman.

CHAPTER XI.

Mrs. Dorriman was very quiet all the long journey, with the tedious changes going to Renton. Her heart was overflowing. Her sweet disposition, which had enabled her so completely to forgive the wrong done her about Inchbrae by the brother she was going to see, made her fearful lest some disclosures now might give Mr. Stevens an unfavourable idea of Mr. Sandford.

She knew that there was no liking to begin with, and that the man she was learning every day to love more and more resented for her, more than she did now for herself, the unfair treatment she had met with at her brother's hands.

Mr. Stevens was very upright and very honourable, and he conceived, as most people would, that for any man to take advantage of a woman's ignorance of business matters, and deceive her for his own particular benefit, was iniquitous; and Mrs. Dorriman, with her great unselfishness and humility, her anxiety to do right at any cost to herself, ought to have been sacred.

The nearness of the relationship only made it all the worse; and he could not bear to hear his Anne—as he now called her—extenuating and pleading for this brother.

She learned to understand this, and to shun the subject; but it was impossible for her, now that she was whirling along this same road, not to feel intensely the contrast between then and now. The comfort of having everything so quietly arranged for her—to have no anxieties because *he* was looking after everything—was quite indescribable. One terrible Junction, where she had formerly stood in despair, and had been shouted at by porters, and pushed here and there, lived in her memory as a sort of gulf, out of which the kind hand of Providence alone sent her in the right direction, now seemed a quiet enough station, as, with her hand underneath his arm, he went quietly round and ordered the porters about in a manner she never would have dared to do.

Then they arrived at Renton, and went on, leaving Jean, by her own wish, to follow on foot with Christie, who proclaimed herself tired to death of sitting still, and longing to take "a bit walk."

"And this was the place, and this the house, Mr. Sandford brought her to when he got her to leave Inchbrae?" said Christie, looking at the square unpretending ugly house in front of her. "Jean, my woman, you did not say a word too much, you did na say enough."

"It is comfortable inside," said Jean.

"Like enough," answered Christie; "but you do not know, and I do know, the home she came from."

Arrived at the house, Jean's air of being at home was very amusing, even to Margaret, who had that indefinable sense of something impending which comes to us all at times.

She was conscious herself of understanding nothing fully, and she was trying to guard herself against drifting into a selfish self-absorption. To her the place was full of very painful memories. Here she had first seen Mr. Drayton, and, with Grace, had laughed over those shattered dreams about a coming prince—who presented himself in middle-aged plainness. It seemed to her that nothing was changed, and she half expected to see Grace flutter downstairs, with saucy speeches and careless wilful disregard of Mr. Sandford's wishes.

By-and-bye they had dinner. Mrs. Dorriman had seen Mr. Sandford, who was not suffering that night, and who wished to see Margaret after dinner. Mr. Stevens had seen them to the door, and had gone home to the place he had taken, with the works, in which formerly Mr. Drayton had been mixed up.

"Margaret, my dear," said Mrs. Dorriman, when the quiet dinner had come to an end, "Mr. Stevens wants us to go and see his house to-morrow. He is so kind; he wants to know if I should like to alter things—fancy its having come to this! that I am to alter things if I like—it is quite wonderful!"

"It is wonderful that you take all this as you do," said Margaret, kindly. "I wish I could put a little conceit into you, or a little of my own selfishness. I should be better with less."

"You selfish! My dear Margaret, you only think so because you have not many other people to think of just now. Selfish! Why a selfish woman would have kept all that money. How much good you have done with it!"

"That is not the same thing, auntie dear; parting with money I disliked using, while I was assured of all comforts and necessaries without it, did not involve any sacrifice. It is like giving away when you are so rich you cannot miss it; but I know that I am inclined to think constantly of myself and of my own convictions about things; even your example has not cured me, though I own it has done me good."

"My example? My dear Margaret, I never thought of setting an example to any one!"

"No, you never think of yourself in any way, and that is why you are so delightfully unselfish," and Margaret, not demonstrative as a rule, rose and kissed her.

Mr. Sandford did not seem so much changed to Margaret's inexperienced eyes; his voice, much lower than before, was still harsh. He looked long at Margaret, and said, as though more to himself than her,

"I was right; the likeness is there."

Margaret tried to talk to him, but there was something so mournful, so terribly sad in his expression, that she was more than half frightened, and was herself nearly moved to tears.

"I wish you to say 'Forgive,'" he said, in a very hesitating manner, "and I wish you to say good-bye. I want to pass from you, who are so like *her*, before you know my story. Will you forgive?"

"I do forgive." said Margaret; "do not think that I blame you for all. Grace was very wilful, and I ... made an idol and dashed myself nearly to pieces against it; my judgment was obscured and I also did wrong."

"You are kind to say this—there is some justice in it; but I have never forgiven myself; I have ruined your life; what is there now to do? I have nothing in my power; I cannot make amends!"

"Have you not heard?" said Margaret, while a lovely colour stole into her face and made it still more beautiful; "I have love offered me and I have love to give. Sir Albert...."

"Thank God!" he said, fervently, and, exhausted by his own emotion, he closed his eyes.

Margaret stood up and looked down upon him; the intensest pity for a man so lonely and so despairing filled her.

"Oh!" she said, in a low, penetrating voice, "take comfort; I am weak and very full of faults, and I forgive. There is a Higher to look to, to ask forgiveness from. If I can forgive, who am like yourself——" she paused, frightened; watching his face, she saw an expression of agony pass over it.

"I will come again," she said, hurriedly, and went to call his servant.

She waited late that night but only heard of his being better, and then went herself to rest.

Next day Mr. Stevens came, and remained talking to Mrs. Dorriman. Mr. Sandford was much better, and they were to go and see Mrs. Dorriman's future home.

It was certainly an instance of there being two sides to every question. Margaret, who had never driven far while at Renton, and who only knew the grimy streets outside Mr. Sandford's circumscribed grounds, was astonished to find herself driving out into the country, with a broad river full of ships, life, colour, and movement. The carriage turned into a broad avenue of trees, and the grounds were well kept and large, the house charming and full of lovely things. Mrs. Dorriman was quite delighted with it all. She had a womanly element of loving good domestic arrangements, and thought she had never seen a house more conveniently planned or more thoroughly delightful. Even the smoke did not seem to penetrate so far as this abode of bliss, though Mr. Stevens, who was nothing if not honest, assured her it did under the influence of certain winds.

"You cannot expect otherwise so near a manufacturing town."

"Then," said Mrs. Dorriman, in so delighted a state of mind, and seeing everything so completely *couleur de rose*, "before very long there will very likely not be any smoke, it will all be consumed," a supposition proving clearly enough that she was unreasonably hopeful, since doing it is economical and is said to be easy, and is never done.

They were a little alarmed to see that the doctor was watching for their arrival.

"Mr. Sandford had rather a bad attack but is better again. He wishes to see you all if you will go to his room. If he is much agitated I have some drops I should like to give myself, so I will wait here, if you please."

He said all this in a matter-of-fact tone, strangely different from the state of excitement poor Mrs. Dorriman was in.

"Does Mr. Sandford wish to see me?" asked Mr. Stevens.

"You were particularly mentioned," answered the doctor.

Mr. Sandford was sitting in front of his writing-table, his right hand shading his face.

"I am sorry you have been ill, brother," said Mrs. Dorriman, gently.

He took no notice, and did not raise his head.

"Is Christie here?" he asked.

There was a pause, and the three stood full of a suppressed agitation. Even Mr. Stevens, as he looked on the terrible signs of suffering on the haggard and miserable face before him, was conscious of a far softer and more forgiving spirit.

Christie came at once and stood near the door, a triumphant expression upon her features.

Still keeping his hand so, partly screening his face, Mr. Sandford began to speak in a low clear distinct voice, without inflections or emphasis—a voice that seemed hardly to belong to him.

"Anne, I have wronged you most. I must speak to you, and the others must hear.

"You have sometimes, in old days ... you used often to ask me who my father's first wife was—you remember? Who my mother was?"

"I remember."

"My father, our father, was only married once, Anne, and your mother was the only wife he ever had."

There was a breathless silence—Mrs. Dorriman not fully understanding the purport of his words.

"Therefore," continued Mr. Sandford in a hard tone, speaking almost as one under the influence of some powerful narcotic, "I have no rights, no name. I am not the heir, I never was the master of Sandford!"

"But you are my father's son?" exclaimed Mrs. Dorriman in a tone of intense suspense.

"I am—but, Anne, I am his nameless son. He never married my mother. Now do you understand?"

Mrs. Dorriman turned to Mr. Stevens, her face pale, she was trembling. She was evidently intensely surprised. He took her hand in his and spoke to her, in a low voice, reassuring words.

"Before you all judge me, hear me!" continued the unhappy man, "for my temptation was great and my trial a terrible one!

"As the only son—brought up unchecked and with power in my hands—it was not till I was nearly twenty-five, madly in love with my wife, that my father told me the truth.

"My God! how I suffered! My father always intended to tell me but he dreaded a scene and put it off always. I think *she* knew, and I was afraid of her!"—he indicated Christie with his hand.

"Do you think that if I had known I would have stood by and seen ill done till her?" and Christie's wrinkled old face glowed with passion. "I had no proof, but I thought my own thoughts. Your mother was a neighbour on the hill-side and she went away; she came back with her bairn at her breast and never a wedding-ring, and she greeted and greeted. A happy wife is proud of her man, she never spoke of hers, she just dwined and died; and your father, a young young man, came home and saw her on her death-bed. 'I'll care for the bairn,' he kept saying in my hearing, and you was moved to the big house. He grieved, for he was kind-hearted enough—but weak, weak as a bracken-bough." Christie stopped short, and a dead silence reigned in the room.

"When I went to my father and told him that I loved Margaret Rivers (and Heaven knows how I loved her!) he answered that I *must* have known this. The facts had been so impressed on his own mind that he imagined I *must* somehow have known them.

"Day after day I renewed my prayers—only to be refused. The strain upon him, the incessant agitation, all acted unfavourably upon him, and the last violent scene we had together ended in his having a paralytic shock, so severe that he lost all power of speech. The terror and misery of it all I still remember, then suddenly it came before me that, as no one knew this dread secret, I might take possession. I spent hours looking through his papers, but I found no proof against me.

"Colonel Rivers had gone to India with his daughters. I followed him there, and married the only woman I ever loved, only to lose her a short time afterwards. I went about nearly mad. I threw up the appointment in a merchant's house I had, and I came back. My father had grown feebler, but at times I was afraid he might rally sufficiently to tell you, Anne, about it. For this reason I sent you from home, and, as we always hate where we have injured, I hated you, and hurried your marriage to get you safe and away from my sight—you were a perpetual reproach to me.

"Then one day your husband found some papers. He was embarrassed and hampered, and I lent him money. He was not a good man of business, and I found it easy to lead him to do what I thought best—but it was equally easy for the next comer to make him do exactly the reverse. In all his difficulties his ruling wish was to put you beyond the reach of adversity, to make you independent. But he only succeeded partly. When he found those papers he came to me and said he had found some curious letters. They were letters from my father to my mother, and, had he read them, he would have known all; but he was an honourable fellow, and, having accidentally seen one and been amused by the spelling, he did not read any more. I was afraid of being too eager, and, before he could give them, he was taken ill and died, and you have those letters now, Anne; they are in that box some instinct, I suppose, made you keep."

He lay back now exhausted—nothing save Mr. Stevens's sustaining hand had kept Mrs. Dorriman quiet. She was fearfully agitated: the cruel wrongs heaped upon her, the long years of a dependence which had galled her so terribly—everything came before her. Mr. Stevens, passing his arm round her, took her out of the room; he saw she could bear no more, she was overwrought.

"Mr. Sandford opened his eyes, and saw her going.

"Ah!" he said, bitterly, "at last I have driven her from my side, even her patient spirit is at length roused. Margaret."

"Yes," she answered, in a constrained voice.

"You are condemning me also."

She could not speak.

The times without number that she had seen him violent and abusive to poor Mrs. Dorriman, the cruel sting that being at his mercy had always been to the poor woman, the imposture, everything bewildered and shocked her.

Mr. Stevens went back, Christie still leaned against the door like a statue.

"How your fraud was successful, I cannot understand," he said, curtly.

"Who was there to ask any questions? Who was to know what had passed?" asked Mr. Sandford; "I had nothing to prove. The result of my father's deception was to make all easy. As I had lived with him, been accepted as his legitimate son during his lifetime, during the time when he might have spoken, why should I not be accepted as his legitimate son when speech was denied him? There were no papers to prove or disprove anything, I was asked to produce no baptismal certificate, and no one thought of questioning me about my mother's marriage certificate.

"But now you know all, take what steps you like to proclaim me to the world an impostor—what signifies it to me? No one can deny me the six feet of earth which is all I shall want directly."

"Sir," said Christie, "when you sold the place was it for fear of a judgment if you lived in it?"

"Sold the place! How could I live in the place to be reminded at every turn that it was not really mine? Every tree, every shrub, seemed to be a witness against me. I grew to loathe the place."

"And what made you think I knew anything?"

"Because your father was so much with mine," he answered slowly; "I never was sure, but I sometimes fancied he knew something."

"He knew nothing, but he did guess; he said, when you sold the place, it was strange, that a man that was well-to-do would not sell a family-place without a strong reason.... But my father was right in what he said," she exclaimed, her eyes becoming brilliant as she saw the fulfilment of his prophecy coming nearer and nearer; "he said you would have your own, my dear, and you have it now!"

She spoke as though Mrs. Dorriman were still present.

Margaret saw that Mr. Sandford was almost past consciousness, and she hurried them away leaving him alone with the doctor, whom she summoned.

Mrs. Dorriman, who for so long now had been kept out of her rights, was quite overwhelmed by this sudden reversion of all her accustomed conclusions; all the long years of her dependence had so nearly crushed her spirit that it was difficult for her mind to grasp her present position. Mr. Stevens was full of patience.

"And the place is sold!" she said, with a sudden sense of not being able to have it, in spite of all.

"I think we can get the man who bought it to give it up," said Mr. Stevens; "we will try at any rate."

She was crying bitterly; she remembered her father's gentle indecision, even about trifles, and indeed her youth would have been far, far happier had he only been able to stand against his son's overbearing temper; but the knowledge of the wrong he had done him made him give in to him. He had been a man who hated anything that disturbed his tranquillity, and only when obliged and forced to do so had he told his son the truth. The effect of this blow was terrible. To have been allowed to grow up looking upon his position as certain, and, just when he was most anxious to have a fair future to offer to the Margaret Rivers he worshipped, to have everything swept away from under his feet, nearly turned his brain.

Mrs. Dorriman could not see her brother at any rate then, and Mr. Stevens did not press her to do so. He knew that the doctor did not think there was any immediate danger, he was to escort her to Inchbrae, fully understanding that she had received too great a shock to recover from immediately.

When she asked Margaret to return with her, as a matter of course, she was surprised, almost hurt, by her refusal.

"I feel that you have happiness in prospect, auntie darling," Margaret answered; "but this most unhappy man! Oh, do not look so grieved! I must do what I feel right. I cannot leave him to face this remorse, and all alone."

"I cannot think of him! I could not see him!" said poor Mrs. Dorriman, with a vehemence utterly foreign to her nature. "Oh, Margaret, if you knew all I suffered in old days!" she stopped, with a sudden sob.

"Do not think that I do not sympathise with you fully and entirely; it is a terrible position; he has injured you, and it has been most cruel; but, auntie, do not let him do you further injury, for there is a further injury that this may do you, a greater wrong!"

Mrs. Dorriman hurriedly swept away her tears that were blinding her, and gazed at Margaret with blank astonishment.

"A further injury, Margaret! What further injury can be left? I have suffered surely enough at his hands?"

"Oh!" exclaimed Margaret, passionately. "Do you not see—can you not feel—that if you allow this to rankle in your mind; if you allow the sweetness of your nature to be turned to gall; if your soul suffers, and that you say it is not possible to forgive—there will be a deeper injury?"

She stopped and left her, and poor Mrs. Dorriman stood looking after her, as though expecting her to return.

Once before she had had a bitter struggle, and she had forgiven. She went to her room, where all was ready for her departure, and she shut herself in....

Blank and desolate was Mr. Sandford's room. He allowed no one to come near him. He sent away Margaret, though she had insisted on bringing him food, and had tried to talk to him.

He sat long hours suffering acutely both physically and mentally. He seemed only now more fully to realise what a crime his was. His sister's character, in his eyes so feeble, was, he had conceived, unfitted for the position she should have held; and this was his own excuse to himself when conscience asserted itself, or rather tried to do so.

They had all left him, he thought. There had been a bustle and a movement in the hall, and he had heard wheels.

The light was waning fast over the room, by the shadow of twilight, in which his face looked wan and white.

He knew that his hours were numbered, and he wished to pray; but he had no habit of prayer; he had always been afraid....

How he was suffering! His heart beat as though each stroke would burst it.

The door opened very slowly, and he started up. Who was the intruder? Who was it that came to mock his sufferings?

Then a gentle voice spoke out of the dim and fading light—"Brother!" and Mrs. Dorriman came up and knelt down by his side.

"I have been wrong," she said. "I thought only of myself, and I did not realise your wrongs. Once again I come to say forgive, as I hope for forgiveness myself."

Her voice died away. She heard him say fervently, in a very low voice, "Thank God!" and she went on—

"But while I do wish you to know this—to try and forget the wrong done to me—there is another to turn to, to ask for forgiveness from."

She felt his hand clasp hers; and as in a dream came from his lips that first prayer of childhood—"Our Father!"

She left him after a while; but she did not go away that night.

Next day his servant, who slept in the little ante-room, saw that he had been busy writing, and then laid down and was now sleeping.

The doctor came and saw him, and directed that some one should stay beside him.

The hours went on, but Christie sitting there saw no change, only a greater stillness seemed to fill the room.

Then suddenly she saw that the sleep was the eternal sleep which knows no waking here.

Mrs. Dorriman at Inchbrae once more suffered long from the effects of all the agitation she had gone through. The last night of Mr. Sandford's life was spent in writing to her, but even to Mr. Stevens she said nothing of the contents of his letter, only comforted by the whispered prayer which was her last remembrance of him. One point she was anxious upon: the recovery of the old place, and whether there was any necessity for letting the world know this painful chapter in the family history.

Mr. Stevens arranged both matters for her. Mr. Sandford, having by will left everything to his sister, she paid the legacy duty for the money, which was found to have accumulated enormously.

Sandford was bought back and refurnished, and, under Mrs. Macfarlane's wing, Mrs. Dorriman again changed her name, and Mr. and Mrs. Stevens Sandford went to the old house. By her express wish there were no great rejoicings—in her heart would remain for a long time that sense of a terrible past, which time only could soften and heal.

But, as a tree nipped and blighted under cruel exposure and an unfavourable soil revives and blossoms when transplanted into genial air, so Mrs. Dorriman's character (we must still call her Dorriman) grew firmer and stronger.

She had much to forget, but love is a great factor, and, as the subject was one which, after the first, Mr. Stevens Sandford would not allow her to dwell upon or talk about, it passed out of her mind by degrees.

She had now a fuller life, sons and daughters clustered round her, and gave her the love she had craved for.

Margaret and her husband were content to live a quiet useful happy life. Her other children did not banish the first from her memory, and her spirits were never high. But she was happy and cheerful. The one constant ruffle on the surface of her smoother sea was her sister.

Grace was always the same Grace—at one moment passionately fond of her husband and lavishing affection and endearment upon him, and the next quarrelling violently with him, and accusing him of almost every sin mentioned in the Decalogue.

Still she kept his affection! She was one of the provoking, irritating, and yet charming people that could sway the passion of a man at will, and she had that strongest claim on the forbearance of a generous man—ill health.

She was a perpetual astonishment to her sister, and often a terrible anxiety.

Margaret's poems were no longer passionate, or even powerful. It has been said, and with a good deal of truth, that the grandest poem, like the sublimest music, springs from human wretchedness, but this applies to poetry set in a minor key.

Margaret's husband gives another reason for her silence. The constant care and thought lavished upon every creature within her radius—she is one of the women who finds her truest happiness in giving it to others.

Christie did not live long; she saw her beloved mistress installed in her old home, and died soon afterwards, happy now right was done.

And Jean? Jean took every one by surprise, and married a hard-working, steady good mechanic at Renton.

They all exclaimed when she announced her marriage, and Mrs. Dorriman said:

"And you, Jean, who think it so dreadful to live near all that smoke, and found it so different to what you had been used to?"

"Eh, ma'am," answered Jean, grinning from ear to ear, "it's no the place, it's the man!"

THE END.

---

[1] Highland married woman's cap.

Milton Keynes UK
Ingram Content Group UK Ltd.
UKHW011143220424
441551UK00007B/773